D0528270

3 4114 00410 2710

THE STRANGER NEXT DOOR

Anna Thompson, a widow with young children, is delighted when someone buys the long-empty home in Northumberland. But the new owner, Daniel Ferguson, is a reclusive single man with disturbing ways. Anna discovers that Daniel is convalescing from serious injuries. She comes to know and like him. They help one another, and find more than simple friendship. Then Daniel's ex-fiancée arrives to shatter Anna's hopes. It will take strong action by Daniel to restore them . . .

JANE BLAKE

THE STRANGER NEXT DOOR

Complete and Unabridged

LINFORD
Leicester

First published in Great Britain in 2008

First Linford Edition
published 2009

British Library CIP Data

Blake, Jane.
  The stranger next door
  1. Love stories.
  2. Large type books.
  I. Title
  823.9'2–dc22

  ISBN 978–1–84782–641–1

Published by
F. A. Thorpe (Publishing)
Anstey, Leicestershire

Set by Words & Graphics Ltd.
Anstey, Leicestershire
Printed and bound in Great Britain by
T. J. International Ltd., Padstow, Cornwall

This book is printed on acid-free paper

1

Anna was pleased, very pleased. It was excellent news that *Moorside*, the house next door to her own, had been sold at last. It had stood empty far too long.

From the kitchen window, as she stood at the sink, her hands working automatically, she could just see a corner of *Moorside*, the corner where ivy covered the stuccoed wall. Her eyes moved on to the dense thicket of trees and shrubs at the bottom of what the estate agent's blurb laughably called 'the naturalistic garden'. Primeval forest, more like. The house really did have a lot of wild land attached to it.

She just hoped the new owners were keen gardeners, and would get the wilderness back under control. It had been far too much for the Rutherfords, the elderly couple who had lived there previously for so many years. No wonder they had given up at last and fled to the sanctuary of the town.

What she longed for most of all, though, was just to see signs of life again next door. People and lights. Children's voices, too, hopefully, and the prospect of company for her own two little rascals. It had been far too quiet for far too long. It was good to know things were about to change at last. She smiled with satisfaction and turned towards the table.

'Lisa! Tom! Lunch!'

Over their meal she told the children what she had learned that morning in the village, which wasn't actually very much.

'Are the new people from the village?' Lisa, a serious-minded seven-year-old, wanted to know.

'I don't know for sure, but I don't think so. Mrs Matthews in the post office would have said if they were.'

'How many boys have they got?' five-year-old Tom asked.

Anna laughed. 'I have no idea! Sorry. All I know, really, is that someone has bought *Moorside* at last, and I'm very pleased they have.'

'Boys!' Lisa scoffed with derision. 'Who wants any more of them?'

'I do,' Tom declared. 'I want someone to play football with.'

'Girls play as well, Tom,' Anna pointed out.

'Not very well, though,' he pointed out, in return.

Anna smiled. She was pleased her daughter didn't try to crush Tom with some weighty riposte. Polite disagreement was a very welcome change.

'When will the new people move in?' Lisa asked.

Anna shook her head. 'Soon, I hope. It would be nice if it happened during the summer holidays, wouldn't it?'

'It depends,' Lisa said judiciously. 'We might not like them.'

'Lisa! Of course we'll like them. We'll be good neighbours, too. Especially at first, they might want some help.'

Anna didn't see a removal van arrive, but a couple of weeks later she did notice a small, white rental van in the front drive. A woman got out of the driver's door and entered the house. A man appeared briefly on the porch. The front door shut again.

So they must have moved in, Anna thought. Good. Excellent, in fact! In a day or two she would go round and introduce herself, and see if they had everything they needed. There was always something missing or forgotten when you moved house, something not there when you needed it, or not where it ought to be. It happened.

Fortunately, when they'd moved here, Bob had been well, and his usually efficient, energetic self. He'd seen to almost everything. He'd done it very well, too, as he did most things before he became ill.

She blinked away a surprise tear. More followed. She grimaced and smoothed them away with the back of her hand. Tears. They still came from nowhere, to take her by surprise and to torment her, even after three long years.

At times she could still hear and see Bob. At times it was as if he'd just popped out for half-an-hour. But most of the time it wasn't. Not now. It was over. She knew, deep inside, finally, that she wouldn't see Bob again in this life.

She ought to move. Give herself a fresh start. The children, too. But she didn't know if she would ever be able to move again without Bob to take charge.

Not that she really wanted to move anyway. Branton was a good place to live and to bring up children. She just wished Bob were still here to share it all with her.

2

There were lights that evening in *Moorside*. Not many, but one or two. Someone was home. Anna kept her eyes open but saw no-one. She didn't the next day either. It seemed strange. Disappointing, as well. Obviously, there were no children. Not yet, anyway. Strange, too, that she hadn't seen a big removal van. Just that small, white rental van. Perhaps it was to be a staged move? One person first. The rest, and their belongings, to follow.

On the third day she walked round to *Moorside* to introduce herself. She rang the doorbell but no-one answered. Someone was home, though. She knew that. She could hear them, bumping and banging about.

She tried again and waited a couple more minutes, with the same result. They must be preoccupied, she decided.

It seemed odd, though, that the curtains on the bay window at the front of the house were closed. These houses faced north. It was at the back, facing south, where you needed blinds or closed curtains when the sun was strong.

She walked away. At the front gate she turned and glanced again at the house. Her eyes strayed to the bedroom window. The curtains there were closed, too, but one swayed slightly, as if someone had moved it aside and then hurriedly let go.

It's none of my business, she told herself sternly, as she walked back to her own house. I really don't want to seem nosy. All the same, it's a bit odd.

'Did you meet them, Mum?' Lisa asked when she got home.

'No, not yet. I went round but I don't think they were up at the time. Probably they're worn out by the upheaval of moving.'

Lisa shrugged. 'They can't have children, can they?' she said, making clear what really mattered. 'Children wouldn't still be in bed.'

Anna smiled. 'Probably not, no. Not unless they're children very different to you and Tom.'

Lisa was right, she thought. Children would be up and about. And people with children couldn't possibly be in bed in the middle of the day, their curtains still closed. That wouldn't work at all.

She asked Mrs Matthews in the post office what she knew of the new people.

'Nothing.' Mrs Matthews shook her head. Then she consulted a card and added, 'A Mr Ferguson is living there, apparently, according to this change-of-address card. But that's all I know.'

'It doesn't say where he's come from, or anything else?'

'Not even that. Just his name. There's nothing else on it.'

'Oh, well,' Anna said with a sigh. 'No doubt I'll meet them eventually.'

'You've not seen anything of them?'

'Not a thing. Just that first day I caught a glimpse of a woman going inside, and a man ahead of her. But nothing since. I've been round a couple of times but no-one answered the door.'

'They must have been out.'

'Possibly,' Anna agreed, though she didn't think so. 'Right. I must be off. Tom will be wondering where his next meal's coming from.'

By then, though, Anna was beginning to wonder. She tried to put the growing unease out of her mind as she made her way home.

'Are you two still in the house, on a beautiful day like this?' she demanded when she reached home. 'Saturday, as well. What on earth are you doing?'

'Playing,' Tom said grumpily.

'I can see that. But why don't you play in the garden? Lisa, don't you want to be outside?'

'Not really.'

Anna shook her head and went into the kitchen to unload the shopping. They were in a funny mood, the pair of them. She didn't know what had got into them.

Oh, well. She would do a bit around the house, and then they could all go out for a walk in the afternoon.

Her eyes fell wistfully on the corner of the garage she could see from the kitchen window. She thought of the car sitting there, unused since Bob had had to give up driving. She should sell it.

Realistically, that's what she should do. It was only deteriorating, and losing value, sitting there.

No! she said to herself defiantly. One of these days she was going to learn to drive. Then watch out! She would be away to the supermarket in the town with the best of them. Maybe a part-time job, as well. She could do that now Tom was in school.

Bob had been going to teach her to drive. In fact, he'd already started. Shown her the basics. Then advice from friends had suggested it might be better, quicker and easier, to take proper lessons before she developed bad driving habits.

That had made sense, but the proper

driving lessons had never started. She and Bob had been overtaken by events. Life had happened to them while they were busy making plans, as somebody famous had once said. John Lennon? Was that who it had been? She rather thought it was.

'Mum! Mum, tell Tom to stop it!'

'Stop it, Tom,' she said automatically, as she began transferring perishables from bag to fridge.

She found herself hoping this little exchange wasn't how they meant to go on for the whole of the holidays. It would be a long six weeks, if it was.

'Did you get any chocolate, Mum?' Tom asked hopefully from somewhere nearby.

'Hello, darling!' She looked round and smiled. 'Just a little bit.' She held up a small mini-bar for him to see. 'You can have one this afternoon, when we go for our walk.'

His face lit up. She leaned down to kiss and hug him.

'Is Lisa going with us?' he asked.

'On our walk? Of course she is.'

'I don't want Lisa to go.'

He was clinging to her now. She had to stop what she was doing. She couldn't push him away and carry on. She just couldn't. There were only the three of them now, and each other was all they had.

'You don't mean that, Tom. I know you don't.'

'Lisa's been mean to me.'

'Well, I'm sure she won't be any more.'

Tom sniffed his doubts.

'Why?' she said. 'What were you two doing while I was out?'

'We were in the garden,' he said, 'and The Secret Wood.'

'The Secret Wood? Where's that?'

'You know. Where nobody goes.'

She was uneasy now, and wondering what he meant. She sat down, put him on her lap and hugged him. He felt hot. He clung to her harder than ever. It wasn't like him. Not at all.

'Oh dear, Tom. What have you two

been up to?' she murmured, sensing something out of the ordinary.

'The man,' Tom said slowly.

She looked at him.

'The man shouted at us. And Lisa said it was my fault, 'cos I wasn't quiet enough. She's been mean to me. I don't want her to go with us for a walk,' he added tearfully.

Anna didn't like what she was hearing, not one little bit. But she had an idea now where they'd been.

'Lisa?'

Lisa was subdued and defiant, stubbornly so, but she admitted they had indeed been in the wood at the bottom of the garden next door. There was nothing unusual about that. It had often been their playground.

'Tom says someone shouted at you?'

Lisa twitched and stretched.

'Is that true, Lisa?' Anna persisted.

Lisa nodded. 'A man,' she said.

'What man?'

'Next door.'

'One of the new people?'

'Yes.'

'Did you see him?'

Lisa shook her head. 'He just shouted and told us to get out. It was Tom's fault,' she added bitterly. 'He's such a baby!'

'I'm not a baby!' Tom protested. 'Am I, Mummy?'

'Of course you're not.'

Anna thought fast. She didn't like what she'd heard. But she had to be careful what she said to the children. She didn't want to frighten them.

'Best to keep out of there, Lisa. It is private property, after all.'

'The Rutherfords never minded.'

'No, but people are different.'

'We've got nowhere to play!' Lisa said bitterly.

'Stay in our garden, darling. Just play here for now.'

It was as if a cloud had blocked the sun from their lives. They didn't need that, Anna thought miserably. She just hoped the problem was no more than it seemed. Face it! she told herself firmly.

The newcomers had every right not to want children they didn't know playing on their land.

'What was the man like, by the way?'

Lisa shrugged. 'I told you. We didn't see him.'

'You just heard him?'

Lisa nodded. Then she yawned, affecting indifference.

But the fact they hadn't seen the man made the incident seem worse to Anna somehow. Sinister, almost.

She shouldn't have left them alone, she decided. And she wouldn't again. She would just have to drag them up and down the hill with her every time she went shopping.

3

Anna's house, *Heather View*, was the last house you came across on the long climb out of the village centre. *Moorside* was close by, but the next house was a good fifty yards further down the hill. And there were no houses at all on the opposite side of the road. In any case, the people Anna knew best all lived in the centre of the village, down in the valley. So sometimes she felt so isolated. And now she was uneasy, worried even.

She fretted another couple of days. Then she called in at the post office to ask Mrs Matthews if she'd heard anything more about the new people next door.

'The new person, you mean.'

Anna stared at her, uncomprehending.

Mrs Matthews shrugged. 'You have a

new neighbour, Anna. But it's not a family. It's one man.'

'A man? On his own?'

Mrs Matthew nodded. 'But I still don't know anything about him yet. Just his name.'

She was a long time getting to sleep that night. It was one of those nights when sleep just wouldn't come, however desperately she sought it. She dozed intermittently. Sometimes she watched in terror, unable to help, as something monstrous but unseen pursued the children with unspeakably evil intent. There were floods, too, vast walls of water threatening to engulf her little house and everyone within it. And bombs. In between these dreadful episodes she lay, increasingly restless, waiting for sleep to take her, as it did eventually for a time.

It was just gone three when she came to the surface, fully awake, on edge. Something had disturbed her. Something was wrong. She lay still, listening hard. For a moment she heard nothing.

Then she heard a clattering noise. Outside. It started. It died. A gruff voice seemed to protest.

Alarmed, she threw back the covers and swung her feet to the floor. She stood up and crossed quickly to the window. Heart racing, she cautiously moved the curtains aside and peered out.

There was a light in the garden next door, behind the big hedge between the houses. It seemed to shine upwards from the ground. Perhaps from a big torch or a lantern. Anna bit her lip. It was the middle of the night. What on earth was going on? Burglars? A break-in? Not with so much noise and light, surely?

Then, as she watched, the outside light on the wall of the neighbouring house came on. She heard a door bang. Someone kicked or flung something metallic. A voice again, angry sounding. Her mysterious neighbour? She shivered.

A smaller light, definitely a hand

torch, moved down the garden. Anna watched, mesmerised. The light came towards a gap in the hedge. Whoever was holding it seemed to place it on the ground. She saw a vague movement and she heard several thuds. She reached for the portable phone and waited, poised to dial the emergency number.

But whoever was there did not come into her garden. Even so, she remained on guard. After half an hour or so, the lights moved back towards the house and disappeared. She heard the sound of a door slamming shut. The external light went out. She waited, but nothing more happened that night.

The next morning, early, Anna opened the back door and stepped out into the garden. For once, she was up before the children. She felt exhausted. But memories of events in the night were fresh, and she needed to know what had been going on.

Part of it was soon clear. Where a gap in the hedge had been there was now a barrier of timber and wire, a roughly constructed section of fence. The children would not be using that route to *The Secret Wood* any more.

She made her way thoughtfully back to the kitchen. As she climbed the steps leading from the lawn to the patio at the rear of the house, she glanced across at Moorside. For a moment, she felt someone was watching her from an upstairs window. Someone was stood well back from the window, but they were watching her. She was sure of it.

She took the children down to see family friends, the Shepherds, in the village later that morning. Lisa and Tom were eager to go, and for Anna, too, the visit made a welcome break.

Derek Shepherd opened the door. 'Well, look who's here!' he boomed cheerfully. 'The Barbarian Hordes in person. Come in, come in!'

'Thank you — I think!' Anna smiled. 'On holiday, Derek? I didn't expect to see you here. I hope we're not intruding?'

'Or you wouldn't have come? I know, I know! I'm not your favourite man, am I?'

'Oh, Derek! Don't be so silly.'

She reached up to kiss him on the cheek. He hugged her in return.

Meanwhile, Lisa and Tom had charged into the house, looking for the Shepherds' two boys, David and Peter.

'Where's Pippa?' Anna asked as Derek led her through to the kitchen.

'She's just popped out to the shop. She'll not be a minute.'

'Derek, you've not planned a family day out, have you? I wouldn't have dropped in . . . '

'Nonsense! You're always welcome here, Anna. You and the kids. You should know that.'

'You have, haven't you? You've planned a day out?'

'Only to the beach. Now you lot can come, as well.'

'Oh, we couldn't . . . '

'You could, and you can,' he said firmly. 'As soon as Pippa's back from the shop, we'll get organised. You can help her make sandwiches. I'll fill a flask.'

She grimaced. She felt her face twisting with embarrassment. She hated to be a burden, or a gatecrasher.

'You do know, don't you?' Derek said anxiously.

'Know what?' she asked with alarm.

'How to make sandwiches? I'm sure Pippa won't mind showing you if you don't. In fact, I could show you myself if I wasn't going to be so busy boiling the kettle and filling the flask.'

She smiled, reluctantly.

'At last!' Derek said thankfully. 'A smile. Hallelujah!'

The Shepherds were old friends of Anna's and her late husband's. They knew Anna well, and had been a great help in the turmoil of Bob's illness and in the months afterwards. So it wasn't easy to hold them at bay.

★ ★ ★

'Is anything wrong, Anna?' Pippa asked, as they sat together on the beach, watching Derek at a safe distance being covered with sand by the children.

'Wrong? No.'

'Managing all right?'

'Oh, Pippa! Stop it. I'm perfectly all right, thank you. Nothing's wrong.'

'So what's wrong?'

Anna glared at her friend. Pippa shrugged and smiled. Anna shook her head with exasperation and reluctantly began to smile, and then to laugh. She couldn't help it.

'You're terrible! Pippa, you really are impossible at times.'

'I know. Derek says the same thing. You can't both be wrong.'

Anna debated saying anything at all. She didn't want to seem hysterical. She didn't want to lean on her friends more than she needed to either. One day she might really need them. She didn't want to have exhausted her credit with them when that day came. All the same . . .

'I've got a new neighbour,' she said.

'Someone's moved into the Rutherfords' old house?'

Anna nodded.

'That's good, isn't it?'

'I was looking forward to new people moving in. We all were. The children were hoping there would be new children to play with, and I just wanted someone living there again.'

'Of course. I know I would hate having an empty house next to me all that time. So?'

'But it's not a family that's moved in. It's not even a couple. It's just one man, and a very strange one at that.'

'Oh? Retired, is he? Elderly? They can be very strange, people who've been living alone for a long time.'

'I don't know.' She looked up and shrugged. 'I've never even seen him. He's been there three weeks, and I've not seen him. Mrs Matthews told me his name, but that's all I know. And he doesn't answer the door to anyone.'

'How strange.'

'I'm uncomfortable about it, Pippa. I don't want to pry, or invade anyone's privacy, but I'm not happy about the situation. I really don't know who I've got living next to me. I don't sleep well. I wake up a lot. And I see lights in his garden, and hear him doing things.'

'What sort of things?'

'Things!' Anna shrugged. 'I don't really know. Except one night he made a fence to plug the gap in the hedge the children have always used to go to the wood.'

'At night? That's odd.'

'It's worse than odd, Pippa. At times I'm really worried. At times I'm frightened. And the children are reluctant to play outside now. They're affected, too.'

When Derek returned from playing in the sea with the children Pippa brought him up to date with what Anna had told her.

'That's no way to go on,' he said, shaking his head. 'He must be a funny fellow.'

Anna agreed but in a way she wished she hadn't said anything. She didn't want them to think her feeble, afraid of shadows.

'I haven't heard anything about him,' Derek said. 'But I'll ask around. And maybe I'll call on him myself. That do?'

Anna nodded and smiled her thanks. She felt better already. Somehow the situation didn't seem such a problem now. They could enjoy the rest of the day.

Derek was as good as his word. But he got no further than Anna had.

'Couldn't get him to the door,' he complained ruefully, when he dropped in to report progress, a couple of days later.

'Strange, isn't it?'

'Very.'

'It's as if he has something to hide.'

'Well . . . ' Derek said judiciously. 'I didn't want to worry you, Anna, but I was thinking that myself. But I'm sure there's some simple explanation.'

'I hope so,' Anna said, although

privately she doubted it.

'Perhaps he just wants to be left alone.'

Indeed that seemed to be the case, although the question why anyone would want that in a place like Branton was itself a puzzle. At the very least, it didn't bode well to have such a neighbour, not in a place where people depended on each other for all sorts of little things. More than ever, Anna wished the Rutherfords had never left. Giving them occasional help with the shopping and the garden no longer seemed a heavy price to pay for their unfailing kindness and courtesy.

'Give me a ring,' Derek instructed, 'if anything happens or you're worried. I'm only a couple of minutes away.'

Anna nodded. But she hoped it wouldn't come to that.

4

A car drew up in the drive of *Moorside*. Anna paused in mowing the lawn to watch. A woman, a middle-aged woman, got out and walked up to the front door. She let herself into the house. Anna blinked hard. Obviously the woman had a key. That was a surprise.

So there was a woman there, as well as a man? No. There couldn't be, surely? Mrs Matthews would have known, unless the woman was just a companion or a friend.

Somehow, though, she couldn't see a man like the one next door having friends. Not the way he carried on. As for a partner . . . ? No, again. No woman would live like that. Then there was the car. She hadn't seen that before.

Then it came to her that she had seen the woman before. Possibly. On the very first day there were signs of life next door she had seen a woman going into the house. Her memory of the woman was hard to recall in detail, but she was pretty sure it had been the same one. So who was she? It was a mystery.

She shrugged and got back to work. She was determined to finish the lawn in one go. Besides, what anyone did next door was none of her business. Mr Ferguson, if that really was his name, could have as many visitors as he liked. He could give them all keys to the house, as well! She didn't care.

Except she did care, and it did matter. *Moorside* was next door to where she and her children lived. That made a difference, a huge difference.

Derek dropped by later. By then, the car next door had gone. 'You've been busy in the garden, I see?' he said with approval.

'Tidying up a bit. That's all. Mowing the meadow that we used to call a lawn. Will you have a cup of tea, Derek?'

'Yes, I will. Thanks.'

She led the way into the kitchen. Derek planted himself down at the big table. She smiled.

'What?' he said. 'What have I done?'

'Nothing!' she assured him, still smiling. 'It's just so nice to see a man sitting there again.'

'Am I in Bob's place? Sorry. I'll shift myself.'

'No, no! Stay exactly where you are.' She put a restraining hand on his shoulder. 'I meant it,' she added. 'It is nice.'

'Aye, well. It's been a difficult few years for you, hasn't it? I know that. You've done very well, Anna. The kids are grand, and you've kept the home together. I admire you. We both do, and I'm sure we're not the only ones in the village that feel like that.'

'Thanks.' She gave a wry smile and shrugged. She was pleased but a little embarrassed. There was no-one to give her little compliments these days. She wasn't used to them.

'How's Pippa?'

'Fine, thanks. She's away at her father's today. She said she was going to drag him to the supermarket in town, to make sure he's got enough food in the house. I wished her luck.'

Anna chuckled. 'She could imagine it wouldn't be straightforward. Pippa's father wasn't the easiest man in the world to tell what to do.'

'And you?' she asked.

'Oh, I'm all right. I would be a lot better if they would give me a decent budget to play with at work. I spend most of my time trying to save money and figuring out ways to make things do, instead of doing them properly.'

Derek was a highways engineer with the County Council. His complaint about budget cuts, year after year, was a familiar gripe.

Over their cup of tea, Derek said, 'I finished the job early today. So I thought I'd drop in on your new neighbour again.'

'Oh? Are you going to?'

'I've been.'

'Really? What happened?'

'Nothing. Just like last time. No-one came to the door.'

'I've still not seen him either,' Anna said with disappointment. She'd hoped *Moorside*'s front door might have opened to a man.

'No signs of life at all,' Derek added, 'though some work's been done recently in the garden.'

'At night. That's when he does it.'

'So you said.' Derek shook his head. 'It's a funny situation, isn't it? The least bit of trouble give me a ring. I'll be up here in a couple of minutes. Don't bother ringing the police. It'll take them an hour or two to get here.'

Anna felt worried now. 'It's not going to come to that, surely?'

'No.' Derek shook his head. 'I'm sure it isn't. I'd like to know who he is, though.'

'Me, too.'

'Well, don't worry. I tell you what I'll do. I'll get on to the estate agent who sold the house. See what they can tell me about the mystery buyer.'

'Would you? Oh, that's a good idea. Why didn't I think of that?'

'Someone must know something about him.' Derek said slowly. 'And that's one place to start. If I run into Eddy Rogers, I'll ask him if he can make some enquiries, as well. He might be only a Special Constable, but he knows the community. There must be someone out there who knows who this man is.'

'There is, actually,' Anna said slowly. 'He had a woman visitor earlier today.'

'Oh? Did she get into the house?'

Anna nodded. 'She seems to have her own key.'

'Did she now! Well, well. There you are, then. That sounds better. Perhaps it's a more normal situation than we were beginning to think. Don't you worry any more.'

Anna smiled. 'Me? Worry?'

She felt a lot better after Derek's visit. She even began to wonder if her worrying might all have been unnecessary.

There was music that night, beautiful, haunting music. For perhaps half an hour a solitary violin whispered and sang through the gardens. For once, Anna didn't mind being kept awake by noise from next door. When it was over she fell asleep, and she slept till morning.

As she dressed, she glanced out of the bedroom window. She was just in time to see a now familiar car pull into the drive of *Moorside*. The woman she had now seen several times got out.

Anna studied her. She looked to be in her mid-forties. Slim. Short, fair hair. Dressed in fawn trousers and a casual red jacket. She was presentable enough, but not a jolly-looking woman. Definitely not a fun-loving, smiling sort of woman, Anna thought. She looked intent and serious. Too much so.

The woman walked round to the back of the car, a small hatchback, lifted the rear door and took out several plastic bags. She'd been supermarket shopping, from the look of it. So, Anna thought, she'd travelled a fair way.

The woman set off towards the front door of the house. Anna wondered if she would stay this time or if she was only visiting again.

* * *

'Mum, can I go and play with Katy today?' Lisa asked over breakfast.

'Yes, if she's in. Shall we phone to see?'

Katy was a friend Lisa didn't see a lot of, but clearly she had risen to the top of the list.

'I'll play with Katy, as well,' Tom announced.

'I don't think so,' Lisa said sharply. 'I really don't think so.'

'I will!' Tom insisted.

'Not today, Tom,' Anna intervened. 'We'll do something different. I don't know what yet, but we will. We'll walk Lisa down to Katy's, if she's in. Then you and I will think of something we can do.'

The school holiday might get to seem a long one this year, Anna thought. She was going to run out of ideas for amusement if she wasn't careful. Still, it was a nice problem to have, being with the children every day. At least it ought to be she thought a shade desperately!

Katy was at home that day. Even better, her mother was thrilled at the prospect of company for her. Anna smiled as the other woman explained her predicament.

'I can't get on with anything. The minute I start, Katy has a little tantrum or announces she's bored. She won't even play in the garden herself. So am I pleased Lisa wants to come!'

After dropping Lisa off in the village, Anna took Tom for a little walk and for an ice-cream. She collected a few things she needed from the village shop. Then it was time for the long slog back up the hill. By then, Tom was worn out and fractious. So it was an exceedingly long haul.

Soon, Anna promised herself, I'm

going to see about driving lessons. I really am. I'll scrape the money together and do it somehow. I need to get that car out of the garage and on to the road. Maybe I'll ask Derek to look at it first. See if it's roadworthy.

The woman visiting *Moorside* was opening her car door as they passed by the front gate.

'Good morning!' Anna called, seizing the moment, ready to introduce herself.

The woman glanced round, gave a curt reply and got into the car, slamming the door shut after her, ending all possibility of conversation.

Anna felt disappointed and humiliated at what was clearly a rebuff. She continued on to her own gate, dragging a weary Tom along after her. By then; the woman had reversed her car through the gate and on to the road. She drove off without giving Anna and Tom another glance.

5

She came awake in a thrashing, violent huddle, her senses overwhelmed by a noise she hadn't heard before. She found herself on her knees beside the bed, listening hard to a loud, staccato crackle becoming a roar. Her heart stopped racing. Her breathing slowed. She got to her feet and moved to the window.

That man! What on earth was he doing now?

She could see next to nothing. Just a couple of dim lights near the bottom of the garden next door.

She shook her head with anger. She knew now what the noise was. She recognised it. Somebody down there was operating a chainsaw. In the middle of the night!

'I'm coming, I'm coming!' she called as Tom began to wail.

None of them was in very good shape the next morning. Broken sleep didn't suit them. Anna knew she was going to have her work cut out to cheer the children up.

'We could go fishing today,' she suggested. 'After breakfast, let's see if we can find the nets we bought last summer. They're in the garage, aren't they, Lisa?'

Lisa nodded but didn't say anything.

'Tom, will you help me look for them?'

Tom slowly chewed at a piece of toast as if he hadn't heard her.

'Tom?'

He looked up. He stared uncomprehending at her.

'Oh, Tom! You're worn out, aren't you? What you need is a good sleep.'

So did she and Lisa, actually. But she knew that going to bed in the daytime wasn't a real solution. What she needed to do was find a way of stopping that dreadful man waking everyone up at night again.

She would have to try harder to meet him. Failing that, she could always send him a letter, she supposed. It seemed ridiculous even to think of doing that to a next-door neighbour, but what else could she do? Ring the police or the district council? Ridiculous, they would think, if not say.

She heard the chainsaw again the next night, and the one after that. Not for a terribly long time, but long enough to ensure that the three of them were exhausted again in the mornings, and for much of the day that followed.

She didn't even bother trying to go to sleep the following night. She waited. She was poised, ready to leap out of bed and do something — anything!

But it didn't happen. Nothing happened. Eventually, exhausted, she fell asleep. She slept soundly. They all did. It was ten the next morning before Anna woke up. Even then, it was only because the doorbell was ringing. Lisa and Tom were still in bed.

'Anna! Is anything wrong?'

She stared, bleary-eyed, at Pippa through the half-open door. 'Wrong?' she said slowly, shaking her head. 'No. Come in, Pippa.'

'Are you ill?'

'No, of course not. Please come in.'

Pippa came inside and turned to look at her with concern. 'Anna, you look terrible. What is it? And don't you dare tell me nothing!'

With some reluctance, Anna brought her up to date. 'I'm exhausted,' she concluded.

'I can see that. Where are the children, by the way?'

'In bed. They're exhausted, too.'

'You'll have to do something, Anna. You can't go on like this.'

Anna felt better already. It was a relief to hear someone else thought as she did.

★　★　★

It was a beautiful, lonely night. She knew it as soon as she woke up. Her

41

room was bathed in brilliant moonlight that eased its way effortlessly through the curtains. Still, too, and quiet.

Or it would have been if somebody not far away had left his chainsaw in the shed.

She grimaced and sat up. How could he do this yet again? She'd hoped it was over, that part of her life where this terrible noise tore her from sleep.

Well, she knew now what she must do. She would make a start first thing in the morning. No more dithering. She would write a note and post it through his letterbox. It would be a start.

If that had no effect, she would contact the Parish Council and the District Council.

She felt so satisfied by drawing up this mental programme of action, and she was so exhausted anyway, that she fell asleep even before whatever was going on next door had finished for the night.

In the morning she wrote the first note and delivered it even before the children were up for breakfast. Right! She thought grimly, and with some satisfaction. If it's war you want, Mister, I'm in the mood.

Pippa said, 'Good for you!' when Anna phoned her. 'That's telling him. Exactly right. What did you say?'

'Not much. Just that the use of a chainsaw in the middle of the night is unacceptable to me and my family, and that we want it to stop immediately. If it doesn't, I said, my next step will be to contact all relevant authorities with a view to seeking a court injunction.'

'Wow!' Pippa said eagerly. 'Did you really say all that?'

'Certainly I did. A bit more, as well, actually.'

'I'm proud of you, Anna. Well done!'

'Thank you, Pippa. Now can you come over to tea this afternoon?'

'Oh, not today. I can't. Sorry. I'm expecting the carpet fitter. Can you come here?'

'To see your new carpet? Certainly. I wouldn't miss it for the world.'

She may have done well in Pippa's eyes, she thought. She had even done well in her own opinion. Made a start, at least. But it hadn't worked.

She lay half-asleep, listening absently to that dreadful noise once again. There was nothing like it. There was nothing that could compare. Why couldn't he just play the violin music at night? As loud as he liked! She didn't mind that. Playing the violin was something she'd long wanted to do herself. Not as much as driving a car, of course. But she would like to be able to do it. Or the fiddle.

But was it a violin or a fiddle she'd heard that time? She couldn't remember. She listened hard, and couldn't hear it at all now. But it wasn't a violin or fiddle now, was it? Neither one. Not tonight.

She sat up, wide awake now. Of course it hadn't been a violin, or a fiddle. It had been a chainsaw — again! But now she couldn't hear it. It had stopped. Very quickly. It seemed as if it had been going no time at all. Strange.

She got out of bed and went to the window. She peered into the gloom. There was a light at the bottom of the garden. But she couldn't hear anything.

She was puzzled. Something was different. She didn't know what, but something wasn't right. Something was wrong, in fact. She felt it strongly. Maybe because there was no noise now to go with the light?

She hesitated. The feeling that something was wrong was too strong to deny. She had to know. She couldn't just return to bed.

She dressed quickly, throwing on jeans and a jumper. Downstairs she pushed her feet into the rubber boots she kept handy near the back door. Then she let herself out. She stood still for a moment, listening, feeling the night chill on her face. Then she set off, senses alert.

There was no noise at all now. Not a sound. No wind even to make the trees whisper and sigh. Nothing. Almost nothing. At first, anyway. Then a distant barn owl hooted. She paused, to listen harder. A faint sound carried to her then. No more than a whisper, a whimper, on the night air, but it came from the trees.

She reached the end of the hedge and stepped over the low fence between the gardens, her eyes on the lamp that seemed to be shining unattended. She called softly, a greeting with a question mark after it. There was a groan in response. She gasped and felt her heart begin to race.

'Are you all right?' she called less tentatively.

There was nothing for a moment. Then she heard a man's voice say, 'No!'

Ordinarily, the response, from an unknown person in the darkness of night, might have frightened her. Now it reassured her. She pressed forward, pushing aside low branches and bushes as she worked her way towards the lamp.

She reached it, a battery-powered,

heavy-duty lamp, and picked it up. She swung round with it and immediately spotted a main laid on his back, with a heavy tree branch across his legs. The dreaded chainsaw lay a few feet away.

'What happened?' she asked, gabbling. 'Are you hurt? Can you move? What can I do?'

He grunted and groaned, and turned his face away from the light. 'Get that darned light out of my face!' he snapped.

That brought her back to reality, and out of shock.

'I take it you can't move your legs?' she said calmly, eyeing the massive branch. 'And you can't move that branch either?'

'That's right,' he said sharply, his face still turned away from her.

'Is anything broken?'

'I don't think so. There would be more pain if . . . It hit me on the head,' he added.

She swallowed hard, forcing herself to think, and to be logical. He was having that effect on her.

'I live next door,' she said. 'I guessed something was wrong. What can I do? Go for help?'

'Not necessary — yet.' He sounded very calm now. Coherent, too. As if consciousness was returning.

'If you can just ease that branch even slightly,' he gasped, 'I'll be able to wriggle out.'

'I can't lift it myself,' she said, wondering if she should phone Derek.

'You need a lever,' he said through gritted teeth. 'A pole or a smaller branch. Stick one end under and ease it up. See if you can find one.'

The first thing she tried was a long thin branch. It snapped. She cast about for something else.

'Try the spade,' he suggested.

She did. But nothing happened.

'It's not long enough,' he said. 'Not enough leverage. Give me that. You find something else.'

She did as he suggested. His manner and voice carried authority. He knew what he was doing.

There would be time later to remind him that maybe he didn't.

She found a fence post. Between them, her with the post and him with the spade, they managed to achieve some leverage. They didn't raise the branch much, if at all, but they were able to ease it up enough to take the weight off his legs. With a lot of effort, and much grunting, he wriggled free.

He lay curled up, gasping from the effort or from pain. She couldn't tell. It could be either. She stood back and waited. She needed to see if he could move his legs.

With a groan, he sat up. Then he held on to her arm and gingerly levered himself to his feet. He stood a moment, flexing his legs and ankles. Then he began to shuffle away. No broken bones, Anna thought with relief.

'Thanks,' he said over his shoulder.

'How does it feel? Anything broken?'

'Probably not, no.'

She couldn't help herself. 'What were you doing?'

'Felling trees.'

'In the night?'

'In the night,' he agreed. 'This way,' he added, taking the lamp from her and turning to head towards the house.

She shrugged and followed. She sensed he resented her questions, and perhaps her presence — or the fact that he'd needed her help.

Well, she resented it, too! She resented everything about this night, and the nights that had preceded it.

She got nothing more from him. At the house, without looking at her, he thanked her again, curtly, and wished her goodnight. She shook her head, dumbfounded that that was seemingly all there was to be for it. No proper explanation. No account of himself. Nothing, really. Not even introductions.

As he turned to mount the steps, the light in the porch caught the side of his face. She stared in horror, and was still staring after him when the door shut, leaving her alone in the night.

6

Thinking about it afterwards, she realised there was a lot she didn't know about the man next door. Nearly everything, in fact.

She sat in the kitchen, nursing a cup of tea and reflecting on the events of an extraordinary night. The clock on the wall said it was nearly three but she didn't feel like even attempting to go back to sleep. There was too much on her mind.

She had caught only the briefest of glimpses of his ruined face but she had been shocked by what she had seen. No wonder he had tried to keep his face turned away from her. The fact that he had done just that suggested, too, that it wasn't a long-standing disfigurement. He was self-conscious about it, and he wouldn't have been if he was used to it.

He wasn't a youngster. Probably

51

forty-ish. By his age, he wouldn't even think about it any more if his face had always been like that. Her guess was that something had happened, and probably not such a long time ago either.

Something must have happened. An accident of some sort? A car crash? Fire? Probably. It looked as if he'd been burned. She winced. How horrible! Poor man.

But her discovery went some way towards explaining his strange behaviour. And there was no getting away from it: his behaviour was strange. Odd. Eccentric even. Unsociable, as well.

Reluctantly, she smiled. Whoever heard of anyone felling trees — pruning, as he'd put it! — during the night? With or without a chainsaw?

Eccentric, then. Certainly. And self-indulgent? Eccentricity alone couldn't excuse his using a chainsaw at night without a care — or, worse, a thought — for the people who lived around him.

But perhaps she'd discovered a

will be knackered. And the brakes have probably seized. It'll want new plugs and points, of course. And an oil change.'

'Not much wrong with it?' Anna said with a grimace.

'No. That's all fixable. I'll come up and have a look. How about th' afternoon?'

'Would you? Oh, thanks, Der That's very good of you.'

'If you want driving lessons,' I said. 'I can recommend Kenny Arm in the village. He's good. Very p .t. He taught me to drive — a fe ears ago now, mind.'

★ ★ ★

'No, Tom! You can't have a ice-cream this morning.'

'But I want one!' he wailed.

Tom wasn't happy. Nor was Lisa, who was aggrieved that she'd missed out on an ice-cream when she was at Katy's.

'Tom always has his way!' Lisa complained bitterly.

'He's not getting it today,' Anna told her firmly.

Tom was about to give further voice to his disappointment when he spotted his friend, Jack, who had just entered the shop with his mother.

'Jack!' he shrieked with great joy, rushing to grapple with the other boy.

'I owe you an ice cream,' Anna said quickly to Lisa. 'I know Tom got one the other day, and you didn't.'

'That's all right, Mum.'

'No, it isn't. Fair's fair. You missed out the other day. But I can't buy you one today without getting one for Tom, as well, and I don't want him to think he's getting one every time we come into the shop.'

'It's all right,' Lisa repeated, giving a little yawn to demonstrate how profoundly uninterested she was now in the whole subject.

Anna gave her a little hug and took her place in the queue at the checkout.

Sometimes, she thought ruefully, being a mum is like it must be chairing a meeting of the UN Security Council.

'Oh, hello!' she said, realising who the woman in front of her was.

The woman turned and stared, unsmiling, before returning her greeting.

'I live in the house next door to *Moorside*,' Anna explained, thinking she might not have been recognised.

'Yes, I know,' the woman responded, before turning to face towards again.

Stung by her indifference, Anna said, 'How is your friend?'

'What?'

'The man who lives next door to me,' Anna said with quiet determination. 'I've seen you visiting. I don't want to be intrusive but I wondered how he is — after the accident.'

'He's very well, thank you.'

Anna gave up at that point. The woman's coldness was beginning to seem so rude as to be almost comic.

After paying at the till, Anna

collected Tom and Lisa and turned to leave the shop. Through the glass door, she saw the woman from the queue standing next to her car, using a mobile. Then, as she and the children left the shop, the woman called to her.

'Excuse me! Could I have a word?'

Anna turned and waited politely.

'I gather that you helped my brother last night?'

'Your brother?'

'He has the house next to you.'

'Oh?' Brother? So that was the nature of the relationship. 'He had an accident,' she added. 'Luckily, I was able to help.'

'So he said. I've just been speaking to him.' The woman waved her mobile. 'When you mentioned 'the accident' in the shop I assumed you were referring to another episode in my brother's life. I didn't know about more recent events.'

Anna waited patiently.

'He wanted me to thank you, and to assure you he's fine. No lasting damage, he says.'

'That's good.'

'Except he's not fine,' the woman added suddenly. 'Not really. He's anything but fine, in fact, as you may have gathered.'

'I don't know . . . '

'He's convalescing,' the woman continued. 'He was seriously injured on active service with the Army overseas, and he was invalided out — if that's the correct phrase,' she added bitterly.

'I didn't know . . . ' Anna began.

'Of course you didn't! No-one here knows. That's the whole point. That's why he's here, in the first place. It's what he wanted.'

Anna kept quiet.

'He wanted seclusion and anonymity. I'm not at all sure that is what's best for him, but it's what he wanted. And my brother is a strong and independent character,' she added almost with a smile. 'He won't be told anything.'

Anna smiled back and nodded. She was beginning to feel heavily overloaded with information she hadn't expected.

'Aspects of his behaviour may seem strange to you, from time to time,' the woman continued. 'I must ask you to overlook them, if you possibly can, for the time being.'

'The only thing that really bothers me,' Anna said, 'is his use of a chainsaw at night. Lately, my children and I have been desperately short of sleep because of it. It really must stop, whatever his problems. I sent him a note to that effect just the other day.'

'Yes. So I discovered.' The woman nodded. 'You don't need to worry any more on that score. There will be no more chain-sawing at night. I'll see to that. There shouldn't have been any in the first place.'

'That's good to know.'

'One problem he has is that he can't sleep at night. Another is that he doesn't like to go out in daylight. But they are no justification for disrupting your life. That will stop.'

'Thank you for that assurance, and for explaining all this to me.'

'I thought we owed you an explanation, as well as our thanks. My brother wants nothing but to be left alone. Given how well, and at what personal cost, he has served his country, I believe he deserves it.'

She glanced at her watch and added, 'Now I must go.'

'One more thing, if you don't mind,' Anna said. 'It's very awkward at times, in such a small community, not knowing who my next-door neighbour is. Can I ask you to infringe the Official Secrets Act again by at least telling me your brother's name?'

The woman frowned, as if she thought Anna's little joke was in terribly poor taste.

'Daniel Ferguson,' she said almost reluctantly. 'And I am his older sister, Miss Ferguson. Elizabeth Ferguson.'

'And I am Mrs Anna Thompson.'

They shook hands.

'Good-day to you, Mrs Thompson.'

'And to you, Miss Ferguson.'

Daniel, she thought. Daniel Ferguson.

Well, that was something. Quite a lot, actually. A name and an explanation. It didn't make the man a good neighbour but it did make him an understandable one. Now she knew what the situation was, she was sure she would be able to cope with it a lot better.

7

The Shepherds came up that afternoon, as arranged. Derek disappeared into the garage for half an hour. The children disappeared into the garden. Pippa helped Anna make and enjoy a pot of tea.

And Pippa came straight to the point. 'Have you seen or heard anything more about your mysterious neighbour?' she asked.

Anna hesitated, not sure how much she could or should disclose.

'You have, haven't you?' Pippa breathed, leaning forward, eyes bright with curiosity. 'Come on! Tell Aunty.'

'Well, I do know a little more, actually. I met his sister this morning. She's the mystery woman visitor, by the way. She told me he's convalescing, after being invalided out of the Army. Daniel, he's called — Daniel Ferguson.'

'How interesting. What else?'

'Well, I have met him now, but only the once, and even then only briefly.'

'And?'

'I didn't get much of an impression. It was dark, and . . . We met in the garden.'

'At night. In the dark. The way you do, yes. Yours or his?'

'Oh, stop it, Pippa! Stop interrogating me.'

'Not until I know everything.'

'You know as much as me already.'

'I think not.' Pippa frowned thoughtfully. 'You're holding something back, and I shan't rest until I know what it is.'

Anna wasn't sure why she didn't just tell Pippa everything. Why not? It wasn't as if she knew very much more anyway.

Partly, she supposed, it was because she'd been impressed by what Elizabeth Ferguson had told her. If her brother, Daniel, had been badly injured in the way she had described, he deserved the peace and quiet he craved. She could

64

respect that. And, much as she loved Pippa, she also knew that once Pippa knew what was going on, half the village would also know.

Daniel, as she was beginning to think of him, wouldn't want that. So Pippa was going to have to make do with an abridged version of the story.

'What about the noise at night — the chain-sawing?' Pippa asked. 'And the rest of it?'

'It seems to have stopped, I'm happy to report.'

'Well, that's something to be thankful for. So all we have to do now is find out what else he does with his time.'

Anna laughed with her, but she was relieved when Derek returned to give Pippa something else to think about.

'How's the car?' Pippa asked.

'It's in decent enough condition.' He turned to Anna and added, 'I could change the battery for you, and the plugs and points. And do an oil change. That would get it going. But I'd recommend letting the garage in the village give it a good going-over. They're pretty good. Besides, it needs an MoT now it's more than three years' old, and it would have to go into the garage for that.'

Anna nodded.

Anna nodded again and smiled. But suddenly she was beginning to wonder how much all this was going to cost. She really was going to have to get a job — if only to pay for the car!

'We've seen the man,' Lisa said, after the Shepherds had gone.

'Hmm?' Anna responded absently. She was torn between worrying about the car and wondering what they could have for tea.

'We have!' Tom insisted.

'What?'

'The man,' Lisa insisted. 'We've seen him. In the garden.'

Anna stopped and turned to look at them. 'The man next door?'

Lisa nodded. 'He didn't look very nice,' she added.

'What was he doing?'

'Don't know.'

'He was in The Secret Wood,' Tom said.

Oh! She wondered if he was still there. Maybe he shouldn't be. Surely he wasn't going to do anything more with that stupid chainsaw?

'Can you two watch TV for five minutes?' she asked. 'I've just remembered something I need to do before tea.'

She hurried, almost ran, down the garden. She just hoped he wasn't foolish enough to be thinking of operating the chainsaw again, or of felling any more trees. There would be time for that when he was well again.

'Hello? Mr Ferguson? Are you there?'

He was. She could hear him moving in the dense undergrowth.

'Hello!' she called again.

'What do you want?'

She blinked. She hadn't really expected a reply, and certainly not one like that. He'd wrong-footed her again.

'My children said you were here, Mr

Ferguson. I just wanted to ask if you were OK after the other night.'

'My sister told you I was. At least, she said she would.'

'Yes. Yes, she did. I was pleased. But I wanted to hear it from the horse's mouth.'

'Just being nosy, you mean?'

She took a deep breath and decided to ignore that comment. 'My name is Anna Thompson. We haven't met — not properly, anyway — but I wanted you to know that. I'm in the phone book, if ever you should want help or advice, or anything.'

'You mean if another tree falls on me?'

'Well, yes. Anything like that. Marauding elephants. Man-eating tigers. Anything. I'd be glad to help.'

He emerged from the bushes, the infamous chainsaw dangling from one hand. He stood some way off, turned sideways. His face didn't seem too bad. On one side, at least, the side she could see.

'If you're going to use that thing again,' she said carefully, 'we really would appreciate it if it was during the daytime. Chainsaws at night make sleeping very difficult.'

'Yes. My sister told me. The noise is nothing to what I'm used to, but I understand what you mean. I apologise for disturbing you, and I thank you again for coming to my rescue.'

'That's OK.'

'I shouldn't have needed your help, but I'm not as strong yet as I thought.'

'You need to be more patient.' She shrugged. 'I hope you like it here,' she added, 'when you get settled in.'

'Perhaps I will. Thank you again.'

She gave him a little smile and turned away to head back to the house. She sensed, rather than saw, him disappearing back into the wood.

He didn't seem so bad after all, she thought, now she'd met him. Reasonably pleasant. He'd made an effort, too, appearing before her like that. Obviously he had problems but hopefully he would overcome them.

It was good, too, to know that his facial disfigurement wasn't total. Just one side. Mainly. That seemed to halve the problem.

It was also good that today he'd broken his rules and come outside in the daylight, instead of confining his wanderings in the garden to the hours of darkness. Appeared before her, too. Coming out into the open like that would have taken courage.

Well, they would just have to see how they got on in future. But at least contact had been made now, and she felt reassured they didn't have a monster or a master criminal living next door to them. That was progress. Pretty good progress.

* * *

'How did it go?' Pippa asked.

'Great! Really well. Terrifying — but exciting, as well.'

'Exciting? Wait till you get on a

70

motorway. Then you'll be able to say that.'

Anna was on a high. She'd only just had her first driving lesson, and she hadn't felt so excited for a long time.

'Kenny said I was doing really well, taking to it easily.' She stopped and peered suspiciously at Pippa. 'What? Do you think he says that to everybody? You do, don't you?'

'Not at all!' Pippa said, trying unsuccessfully to hide a grin. 'If Kenny said that, he meant it. He'll get you through the test in no time.'

'I don't care anyway,' Anna said with a scowl. 'I enjoyed it.'

'Come on — sit down! I'll make you a cup of tea. You must be worn out.'

'No.' Anna held out her quivering hands for inspection. 'Just emotionally, nervously, drained.'

Anna watched gratefully as Pippa put the kettle on and rummaged for tea bags. It was nice to be a guest in her own home. 'How have the kids been?' she asked.

'Better behaved than mine ever are. Very good, in fact. You're doing a wonderful job with them.'

Anna was pleased by the comment. Compliments didn't come her way very often these days. There was no-one to deliver them.

'Thanks for looking after them, Pippa. I'm really very grateful to you and Derek, you know — for everything.'

'Nonsense!'

'Well, I am. Even if it embarrasses you, I want you to know that. You've been wonderful friends to me.'

'Drink your tea and shut up, for goodness' sake!'

'Happily!'

'Oh, I forgot!' Pippa winced and gave an apologetic shrug. 'Derek says the garage told him they'll have the car ready for the weekend. There's not a lot wrong with it, apparently, but it's in a queue, and some of the other jobs are very urgent.'

'That's all right. It's going to be a while before I can use it anyway. I have to learn to drive and get my licence first.'

'Oh, that won't take long. You're a very capable person, Anna. I have every confidence in you.'

'Have you really? I can't think why.'

'Well, you get on with things. You get them done. I admire you for it.'

Anna hoped some of that was true. She hoped it wasn't just flattery.

'It will make a big different to our lives,' she said slowly, thoughtfully. 'We'll be able to get out and about more. Even just doing the shopping will be easier. I hate having to drag the children up and down the hill every time we need a loaf of bread.'

'You'll be able to buy in bulk, as well,' Pippa pointed out. 'And save some money. That'd what we do. Mind you, it must be good exercise, walking up and down the hill. My two need more of that. So do I, for that matter.'

'Not Derek?'

'Oh, he stays wonderfully slim, whatever he does or doesn't do. Whatever he eats, as well. It's not fair.'

Conversation halted while they listened to a burst of laughter from the children in the other room. Anna made as if to get up, and then relaxed back into her chair again. 'I'll leave them to it a bit longer,' she decided.

Pippa smiled. 'Tell me, Anna. Are you still thinking of job hunting when you get your driving licence?'

'I am. Yes. Now Tom's settled in at school, I could do something part-time.'

'What will you do? Any ideas?'

'Not really. It would have to be something local, though. I can't be driving twenty miles there and another twenty back, not for a part-time job.'

'Is it for the money or because you want to get out of the house more?'

'Both, actually. I manage fairly well financially. The insurance paid off the mortgage, which was the main thing. But there isn't much for extras — like running a car. And, yes, I would like to get out and about a bit more, and spend part of my day doing things with other adults.'

'What was it you used to do, Anna?'

'Before the children were born? I worked in a bank. It was a good job, as well. I liked it.'

'Why not see if you can go back? There's lots of part-timers now in jobs like that.'

Anna frowned. 'Yes? I suppose I could contact my old boss. See what he says. Probably not much hope, though.'

'Something will turn up,' Pippa said encouragingly.

Anna smiled gratefully. She admired her friend's confidence. She wouldn't have minded some of it herself.

She hadn't seen or heard much of Daniel Ferguson since their conversation in the garden. Just the occasional glimpse and sounds suggesting work was being done somewhere next door. At least, though, she knew he was out and about in daylight now, not shut away inside the house. That seemed a good thing for them all. Far better for him, and far better than the nocturnal activities that had been so disturbing for her and the children.

She wondered if he was sleeping any better now. She hoped so. She knew from her own experience during Bob's illness how draining insomnia could be. Persistent lack of sleep could leave you in tatters. She had begun to feel as if she was hallucinating. Nothing had seemed real after a time. Perhaps that was how it had been with Daniel. She shouldn't have been so quick to rush to judge and condemn.

★ ★ ★

As Pippa and Derek were leaving late one afternoon, Daniel's sister turned into the drive of *Moorside*. Anna waved her visitors off and then hesitated, uncertain whether to acknowledge the arrival of Elizabeth.

'Good evening!' the other woman called.

'Hello!'

Anna stood by the gate, waiting awkwardly.

'Daniel's groceries,' Elizabeth said, as she pulled supermarket bags out of her car. 'I shall be glad when he can fend for himself again.'

'Oh?'

'Head injuries. He's not allowed to drive for a year — maybe longer.'

'What a nuisance for you both,' Anna said, now it was clear she wouldn't be rebuffed. 'I can't drive either. But I've decided to learn.'

'A mixed blessing,' Elizabeth Ferguson announced, closing the rear door with an emphatic thump. 'Certainly in financial terms. You learn to drive, and then you have to buy a car. And then you have to pay to keep it on the road — not to mention the exorbitant price of petrol these days.'

'Yes?' Anna said uneasily, thinking this was like listening to her father all over again. 'Actually,' she added, 'I do have a car. My late husband's. It's just sitting in the garage, doing nothing.'

'Depreciating by the minute! That's another cost.'

Elizabeth nodded and with a grim expression set off towards her brother's front door. How Daniel must look forward to his big sister's visits, Anna thought with a wry smile as she turned towards her own door.

Still, a little more of the jigsaw puzzle was in place now. Head injuries, though? That didn't sound good. Perhaps she could offer the Fergusons a bit of help once she'd learned to drive. She'd be able to collect groceries for them, if nothing else. Even she ought to be able to do that.

Now, stop it! she told herself sternly. That's enough negativity. Remember what Pippa said: I am a very capable person! Well, maybe. But she needed to learn to drive and get a job to prove it.

8

It was just after tea. Anna was sitting with the children, watching a TV programme about whales singing to each other and generally having a good time in the ocean. Well, Lisa, and to some extent Tom, was watching. But it had been a long, hard day, and Anna had given up really watching and listening. She was quite content just to be with the children, and to doze along in that not-really-quite-awake state that can be so pleasant when you're thoroughly tired.

She heard Tom laugh out loud, and thought she heard Lisa chuckle. She smiled to herself, her eyes still closed.

Then it happened. There was a loud crash. A man was shouting. Smoke filled the air. Someone screamed. Voices all round her. The noise was overwhelming. She fell off the sofa.

Someone grabbed her arm and, shouting, hauled her to her feet.

'Out! Outside — quick!'

'No!' she screamed.

Then she was coughing. She couldn't see. She was half-dragged, half-carried. She felt her legs trailing, smoke. Terrible smoke. Coughing, coughing, coughing!

She was outside. She felt cold air rush into her throat and lungs. She was still coughing. Her eyes were streaming with tears.

The children! She screamed again. She struggled to her knees and then to her feet, in time to see Daniel Ferguson emerge from the front door with Lisa tucked under his arm. Tom was sprawled on the grass beside her. They were on the lawn at the front of the house.

Daniel lowered Lisa to the ground. 'Fire!' he gasped at her. 'In the kitchen!'

Fire? Anna stared, in a daze. Fire? Oh, no!

He threw a mobile to her and gasped,

'Call emergency!' Then he turned and dashed back into the house, slamming the door shut after himself.

She gasped for a moment, still coughing. Then her senses returned. She scrambled over to Tom and Lisa. They were both sprawled on the ground, crying. She gave them a quick hug and grabbed the phone.

Unable to think properly, she called Pippa's number and tried to explain. She broke off, coughing. She heard Pippa shouting questions at her.

'Emergency!' she croaked. 'Fire!'

Then the coughing started again, and she couldn't stop. She dropped the mobile and reached for the children.

'Stay here — together!' she gasped, her voice hoarse, her throat sore. 'I must . . . must help him.'

She staggered to her feet and stumbled towards the front door. A car screamed up the hill and screeched to a halt at the gate. She turned to look, still dazed. Derek leapt out.

'Wait!' he shouted. 'Anna, wait!'

She waited. He grabbed a rug out of the car and rushed towards her.

They entered the house together. Thick, black smoke billowed towards them. Engulfed them. Ahead, she saw a man emerge from the kitchen, slamming the door shut behind himself. Daniel. He had a cloth over his head. He staggered towards them, shouting. 'Out! Outside!'

They grabbed him by the arms and steered him out of the front door, all three coughing violently.

'Don't open the back door!' Daniel growled with what little voice the smoke had left him. 'The flames . . . The . . . '

He gave up, coughing and heaving for breath. Derek held on to him as he lowered himself to the ground.

'It's Daniel, from next door,' Anna gasped. 'What shall we do?'

'Wait!' Derek said grimly. 'It's all we can do. He's right. We can't go back in there.'

The smoke-blackened figure looked

up. 'I broke the water pipes!' he wheezed. 'It might hold the fire back.'

Then he began coughing again, more seriously than ever.

Anna looked at Derek, who shrugged. 'The lads from the fire station will be here soon,' he said.

The local part-time firefighters, he meant. Anna looked at the smoke pouring from the kitchen room, and wondered how much house would be left by the time they arrived. She began to weep.

It could have been worse. That was what everyone said. Bill Meredith, in charge of the firefighters, said it was only the flood of water from the fractured pipes that stopped the fire spreading to the rest of the house. Derek, even more logically, said what a good thing it was that her kitchen was a single-storey extension to the house, rather than an integral part of it.

'No amount of water would have saved the house then,' Derek said. 'The fire would have shot straight up through the ceiling before you even knew it had started.'

It was a gloomy diagnosis, but Anna could see the strength of it. 'The water must have made some difference, though?' she suggested. 'Oh, yes! Given the layout of the house, that was what stopped the fire spreading, that and keeping the doors shut. That man certainly knew what he was doing.'

So Daniel had done the right thing, she thought wearily. His quick-thinking and experience had probably saved them all. How lucky they were that he had been in the garden when smoke started pouring out of the kitchen window. And how lucky he had the wit to do something about it.

'Do you know yet how it started?' Pippa asked.

Anna shook her head. 'The fire-fighters said it was probably electrical, something to do with the socket for the cooker being so old. But they didn't really know.'

'Those older houses all want re-wiring,'

Derek said. 'It's a wonder there aren't more house fires.'

'Lucky that man next door noticed something was wrong,' Pippa pointed out.

Anna nodded and shivered. She didn't like to think about the alternative. 'He was very brave, as well.'

'And sensible,' Derek added. 'Keeping the doors shut while he tried to do something. What a fire likes best of all is plenty of fresh air.'

'The place is a bit of a mess now, though,' Pippa said with a shudder. 'All that water everywhere.'

'It would have been worse without it,' Derek pointed out. 'A lot worse.'

Anna listened without commenting further. Somehow she couldn't think straight. She couldn't think at all, in fact. She was still dazed. All she knew was that her children were safe, here in Pippa's house. And so was she.

'He wouldn't go to the hospital,' Derek said, shaking his head. 'He should have but he refused point blank.

Said he'd spent enough time in hospitals. All the same . . . '

Anna came to with a jolt. 'Daniel?'

'If that's his name. He wasn't in very good shape either. But he just said he was going home. Insisted, in fact.'

Anna felt bad. She hadn't even wondered how Daniel was.

'What's the matter with him, anyway?' Derek asked. 'He looks terrible. His face . . . '

'I'm not sure,' Anna said quickly. 'Some sort of injury when he was in the Army, his sister said. He got badly hurt.'

'Poor devil. Judging by his face, he's been in a fire before.'

'Of course!' Anna whispered, aghast. 'Of course he has. We should help him.'

She stood up.

'Sit down!' Pippa said firmly. 'You're going nowhere tonight. Derek can check on him.'

'My house, as well,' Anna said with growing agitation. 'I must see to my house!'

'Tomorrow,' Pippa repeated firmly. 'We'll start things moving tomorrow.'

The next morning Anna left the children with Pippa and went up to the house with Derek.

Jack Bradbury, one of the part-time firefighters, was sitting outside in his car. He got out when they arrived. 'We've been keeping an eye on it,' he says. 'To make sure it doesn't come back to life.'

'Thanks, Jack.' Derek nodded and stared at the house. 'It is out now?'

'Oh, aye. Completely dead.'

They both looked cautiously at Anna, who had said nothing so far. She was just staring at the ruined kitchen, roofless now, smoke-blackened joists open to the elements. She wiped away a few tears.

'It's just the kitchen, Anna,' Jack said softly. 'It's a mess, right enough, but it could have been worse. The rest of the house is all right. Just a bit of smoke damage that a cost of paint will put right.'

She turned towards him with a rueful smile, the best she could manage. 'You're right,' she said. 'It is a mess.'

'It could have been worse,' Derek reminded her, 'like Jack says.'

'The next person that tells me it could have been worse,' Anna warned, 'I'm going to give him such a clout!'

The two men chuckled with relief. Then they waited. It was her move.

'Oh, it's OK,' she said with a sigh. 'I know you're right, both of you. Come on. Let's have a look inside.'

'Thank you, Jack,' she added, turning back to the firefighter. 'I do appreciate what you and the other men have done.'

'That's all right, Anna,' he said awkwardly. He looked a little embarrassed as he added, 'It's what we do.'

The kitchen was a total ruin. You couldn't say anything else. There was no floor now. And only sky for a ceiling. The plaster from the inner walls had largely gone, too, exposing the bare brickwork. And everything wood or plastic had disappeared, leaving behind a tangle of bare metal and rubble. They stood and stared through the hole where the back door had been.

'It could do with a fresh coat of paint,' Derek said, breaking the silence. 'Jack was right.'

'Oh, Derek!' Anna laughed, almost hysterically. 'You fool!'

He grinned at her. She gave him a playful push.

'There's no point going in there,' he said. 'We'd just get filthy. Let's have a look round the front.'

They walked round to the front of the house and Derek gingerly pushed the door open. Anna stepped ahead of him, and in her anxiety and impatience almost fell into the hall. People had been right, she soon realised. It could have been worse.

There was smoke discoloration and a pungent stench in the hall. And the door leading off it to the kitchen was in a sad state. Otherwise, though, apart from the terrible smell, you would never have guessed what had happened at the rear of the house.

Some of the tension left her as she sped from room to room. No other damage that she could see. She sagged against the living-room wall with relief.

'You all right?' Derek asked quietly.

She nodded. 'It's not so bad, is it?'

He shook his head and gave her an encouraging smile. 'Right, let's sort out what we're going to do.'

She was grateful for Derek's presence, and for his solid, practical nature. He soon had an action plan drawn up.

'First, find your home insurance policy, Anna, and get in touch with the company. Let them know what's happened. And get their permission for us to start clearing up.'

He glanced at his watch. 'Unfortunately, I can't stay myself. I've got a meeting I must go to. But that doesn't matter. I'll get in touch with Gerry Armstrong, the builder, and have him come up to tell you what's possible here. I'll also have a plumber come up

90

to get the water back on.'

Seeing her uncertainty, he added, 'You'll have to manage without a kitchen for a little while but the rest of the house will be liveable in, if that's what you want to do. We can get you a microwave. Put it in the diningroom, or somewhere, for the time being. And you'll have water. Everything you need, in fact.

'Meanwhile,' he added, 'stay with us as long as you like. We're happy to have you.'

'Thank you, Derek. You and Pippa have been really kind. I don't know what I would have done without you.'

It didn't take her long to do what she needed to do. The insurance documents were in the drawer where they should have been. She rang the company. They were efficient. Someone would be there during the day to make a preliminary survey. And she could organise repair work as soon as she liked.

Suddenly she was free. She had nothing more to do for the moment.

She could return to Pippa's, and to the children, and wait for Derek to let her know what he had arranged with the builder.

She stood in the living-room and gazed out of the window at the huge buddleia that was now developing the purple spikes that would soon attract a myriad butterflies. The lawn needed mowing. The delphiniums needed support. The path wanted sweeping. Life was going on, kitchen or no kitchen.

She would return home in the next day or two, she decided. This was where she wanted to be. Derek was right. They could manage here. As soon as the water supply was restored they would come home.

She closed the front door behind her, out of habit giving an extra tug to make sure the sneck had caught properly. Then she smiled and shook her head, realising the futility of locking the front door when the back door no longer existed.

As she made her way to the gate, her

thoughts turned to *Moorside*, and the man next door. I must call, she thought with guilt at how long he had been out of her thoughts. I must see how Daniel is.

9

No-one answered the doorbell. She rang it several times, with the same result. He was out, was the obvious conclusion to draw. For whatever reason, he wasn't at home.

But she didn't believe that for one moment.

She abandoned the front door and made her way round to the back of the house, anxiety building. She no longer cared about trespassing and invading someone's privacy. That was the last thing on her mind.

To her surprise, the lawn and the flower beds at the back of the house were neat and tidy, and colourful, as well. She paused for a moment and studied the massed ranks of lupins and delphiniums, geraniums and sweet williams. She smiled. All that nocturnal gardening! It had done some good.

No-one was about now, though. And there were no tools laid around. No spade carelessly tossed aside. No rake or even a trowel. No washing hanging to dry. No sign, in fact, that anyone lived here at all. Her anxiety heightened. She cast anxious looks around and made her way to the door to the porch at the back of the house.

She knocked but nothing happened, and she heard nothing. She grimaced, hesitated and eventually reached out for the door handle. It turned. The door was unlocked. It opened. Cautiously, she eased it open and called a greeting. No response.

Even more cautiously, but committed now, she made her way into the house. The old-fashioned kitchen with its black range for a fireplace and the heavy metal cupboards from the 1940s was neat and tidy, just as the Rutherfords had left it. Nothing out of place, and nothing changed. She glanced around quickly and moved on, heading deeper into the house.

She found him in the living room at the back of the house. The curtains were closed and the room dark. She wouldn't have realised anyone was there if he hadn't groaned.

She spun round and gasped. In the dim light she made out a heap of something lying on the sofa. Her fingers found the light switch just inside the room. He groaned again when she switched it on.

'Daniel!' she gasped. 'What on earth's wrong?'

There was no need to apologise for her presence, or for anything else. She could see he was shivering, and he was still smoke-blackened from the night before.

She crossed the room and crouched down beside him. She laid the palm of her hand on his forehead. He was hot, burning. He began coughing. At least that stirred him. His eyes focussed on her.

'Are you hurt, Daniel?' she asked.

He just stared.

'I'll phone for an ambulance,' she said, making up her mind.

A hand reached out and grabbed her skirt as she stood up. 'No!' he whispered fiercely.

'You need help,' she said.

'No hospital!' he insisted.

'Your sister, then? I could call her.'

'No.'

He struggled to sit up. She helped him. He nodded his thanks.

He nodded his thanks.

She was at a loss as to what to do for the best. He was obviously quite poorly, but with what she didn't know. Breathing difficulties seemed a large part of it. Exhaustion, too, perhaps. Even the good side of his face seemed very drawn. Probably no injuries, though. Fractures, anyway.

But he was reviving, she realised with hope. He seemed a little better already, a little stronger.

She crossed the room to open the curtains. Then she returned to switch off the light. He gazed at the window, as if surprised to see so much daylight.

'I keep the curtains closed normally,' he said in a stronger voice, and more as an observation than a complaint.

'It's not a normal day, Daniel,' she said gently.

He nodded.

She sat down near him. 'Daniel, I came to thank you for what you did yesterday. You saved our lives — and the house. I'm sorry I just let myself in, but there was no answer and I was worried about you.'

'That's all right.' He shrugged. 'You've seen me anyway. You know what I look like.'

'A very tired man,' she said firmly, ignoring the underlying message. 'That's what you look like. And you're not very well either. We shouldn't have left you so long on your own.'

'Worried about me?'

'Yes. Worried about you.'

He shook his head as if he couldn't understand it.

'You're not too good, are you,

Daniel? And last night's activities haven't helped. What can I do?'

'I'll be all right,' he wheezed. 'I'm just tired and . . . the smoke,' he added, beginning to cough.

She went to the kitchen and brought him a glass of water. He took it and nodded his thanks. He drank deeply. It seemed to help.

'I'll be all right,' he repeated. 'Don't worry about me. It's the smoke. That's all.'

'Is it bad?'

He shrugged. 'Not as bad as last time,' he said, touching his face with that reflex gesture she was coming to know so well.

She realised then, knowing something of what had happened to him not so very long ago, what an extraordinary thing it had been for him to enter her kitchen.

'You were very brave,' she said quietly, 'and very resourceful. If you hadn't flooded the kitchen, the whole house would have gone up in smoke.'

'Probably.' He nodded. 'How is it now?'

'The kitchen's a ruin, but only the kitchen. The rest of the house is OK, thanks to you. I'll get it fixed. Meanwhile, we're staying in the village with friends. Pippa and Derek.'

'Friends,' he said, nodding again. 'You need them. I lost mine, you know.'

He looked at her so sadly that she almost reached out to hug him.

'I didn't know,' she said softly.

'Oh, yes. I lost them. All of them. There's only me left now.'

Again his fingers traced the pattern of sorrow on his face.

★　★　★

'Anna!'

She turned and smiled. 'Hello, Daniel! Good to see you up and about.'

He was at the fence. He must have heard her. Now he climbed over and came towards her. 'Any progress?'

'We're getting there. The builder from the village is going to start work tomorrow. I came to have a last look at the old kitchen. What's left of it.'

'Is it all coming down?'

She nodded. 'They said it would be best. Easier to clear the site and start again. I don't mind. It was just an added-on extension anyway.'

'So how are you?' she asked, turning to look at him with some anxiety. 'Any better?'

'I'm fine. No worse, anyway,' he said with a grin that seemed to crack his face open. 'Would you like a cup of coffee or tea?'

The question was a surprise, a shock even. She wasn't sure if it really was an invitation.

'I can't . . . They're not going to turn the water on till tomorrow.'

'In my house,' he said firmly. 'I've done enough damage in yours. I don't want to see yours again till it's all fixed up.'

She laughed and nodded. 'Thank you. I'd love a cup of coffee.'

It was as if a door had been opened, a

curtain drawn back. Suddenly she could talk to her next-door neighbour normally, the way good neighbours do. Their difficult past was behind them.

'The children still at your friends?' Daniel asked.

'They are, yes. We're still staying with Derek and Pippa. Tomorrow, though, once the water's turned back on we're coming home, I hope. We can do without a kitchen for a week or two, but we all want to come home.'

'Good.'

'Good?'

'Yes. I prefer it when there are people next door.'

She wondered if he meant them specifically, or people in general. Regardless, she was glad to hear it.

'And you're really all right now?'

He nodded. 'Pretty well.'

He turned away from the kettle, shrugged and added, 'Smoke isn't good for you. I've been reminded.'

'Did you need reminding?'

'No, not really. Not at all, in fact. I've

been living with the knowledge for some time.'

He fingered his face. 'There's always this to remind me,' he said bitterly, 'if ever I'm in danger of forgetting.'

He swung back round and spooned coffee into two mugs. She watched in silence. It was an awkward moment. She didn't know what to say, but she also knew she couldn't leave it there. They needed to get past this very awkward obstacle.

'You've been in a fire before?' she said in a level tone, as he placed the mugs on the table. 'That's what you're telling me?'

'Yes, I suppose it is. I don't need to, though, do I? It's there for all to see.'

'It's not that bad,' she said softly. 'You really don't need to worry about it so much.'

He gave a derisive snort and shook his head. 'Not much!' he said.

'What happened?' she asked. 'Do you want to talk about it? Can you tell me?'

He studied his hands. She wondered

if she had gone too far, pressed too hard.

'A roadside bomb,' he said. 'The vehicle exploded and went up in flames. I was the lucky one. So they said. I got out alive.'

'This was in the Army?'

He nodded.

'Overseas?'

He nodded again and added, 'I can't tell you any more.'

'I don't need to know any more,' she assured him. 'It's in the past, anyway. It's the future that counts. You're finished with the Army now, aren't you?'

'Yeah. At least, they're finished with me. I'm no further use to them.' He shrugged. 'I was close to the end of my service anyway.'

He was carrying quite a load, she thought. Well, maybe he'd come to the right place to live if what he wanted was peace and quiet.

'People here will find out about you, you know.'

He looked startled.

'There's no need to hide yourself away. No point either. At the moment, you're a bit of a mystery. But once folk see you going about, they'll know who you are and soon get used to you.'

'Frightening the kids,' he said bitterly.

'Rubbish! Your face is a bit scarred, it's true, but who's going to worry about that once they get to know you? Come down to the village with me one of these days, Daniel. You'll see I'm right.'

He shrugged non-committally.

'I'll show you around,' she added. 'Take you to the village shop. Teach you how to buy a newspaper, and where to go for a stamp.'

He chuckled.

'OK? When you feel up to it?'

'I'll think about it.'

He walked with her to the front gate.

'There you are!' she heard a voice cry.

She turned. 'Lisa! And have you got Tom, as well?'

'We came to find you.'

'Well, you did. This is Mr Ferguson . . .'

'Daniel,' he said quietly.

'Hello, Daniel!' Lisa said brightly. 'Thank you for saving us all from the fire.'

'I must have frightened you, bursting in like that. I'm sorry.'

Lisa shook her head. 'It was exciting,' she said, 'and now we're getting a new kitchen.'

'Look on the bright side, eh?'

Laughter all round.

Tom, perhaps feeling a little out of it, said, 'Can we play in The Secret Wood again, Daniel?'

'The Secret Wood?' He looked at Anna.

'At the bottom of your garden,' she told him. 'The children used to play there.'

'Oh, yes. Of course you can now I've finished clearing up. I just wanted to make sure it was safe. It is now.'

'See?' Anna said quietly to him. 'That's three of us locals you've met now. Do you think you might grow to like us?'

He smiled. And it was good to see.

10

She was pleased and relieved that the children seemed to have no problem with Daniel, or with how he looked. She was also pleased by how he responded to them, and they to him. Surprised, as well. The children's ready acceptance of him as a new friend seemed to have given him the confidence to relax in their company. He could be quite funny at times. They liked that.

Besides, as she told him herself, he was a hero. That made a difference. He looked blankly at her.

'Lisa made sure all her friends knew who had rescued us from the fire. Those that Derek and Pippa hadn't told already. Within a day or two, everyone in the village must have known.'

'How embarrassing,' Daniel murmured. 'I did nothing. And the kitchen burned down anyway.'

'Only the kitchen, though. Besides, I know how much it must have taken for you to enter a house on fire. You're a hero to me, as well, Daniel Ferguson!'

'Just drop it,' he said curtly.

She did. But she knew he wasn't as mad as he made out.

Repair work on the house began very soon. Gerry Armstrong had taken one look and announced that there was no question: the ruined, smoke-blackened kitchen extension had to come down. The sooner, the better. What was still standing would only get in the way.

'Anyway,' he added with a cheerful grin, 'we can build you a better kitchen than the one you had.'

The surveyor from the insurance company agreed to the proposal readily enough. So work could begin.

Anna waited until the rubble was cleared away. Then she and the children moved back into the house. They were pleased to be back in their own home. Tom stayed in his room for hours, happy to be reunited with his cars and trucks, and the rest of his worldly possessions. Lisa was happy, too, but she wrinkled her nose at the smell. Anna assured her it would soon go now the windows were all open.

She soon found she was short of the very fundamentals of life on the hill now she had no fridge. That would have to be remedied soon, she told herself. She would buy a new fridge and stand it in the hall until the kitchen was rebuilt. Meanwhile, she needed to make a trip into the village. No matter how much food she bought, they never seemed to have enough and there was always something she'd forgotten.

It was an opportunity as well as a chore, an opportunity to acquaint Daniel with the world outside his four walls. And she would do it, she decided, without giving him the chance to think about it and say no. She would just knock on his door and confront him.

With a giggling Lisa and a curious Tom in tow, that's what she did.

'We're all going down to the village,

Daniel, to do a bit of shopping. Will you come with us?'

'Oh, hello! You're back in residence, are you?'

'As of an hour. Yes. Will you come?'

'I don't really . . . '

'Now!' she insisted.

'Now!' Lisa and Tom chorused.

Daniel looked as startled as any rabbit caught in headlights. They were being unfair, Anna knew, but they stood their ground.

'By car?' he queried.

'By walking,' Anna said firmly. 'The time has come.'

'All right,' he said reluctantly, and with a sigh. 'I'll just get my jacket. I suppose a walk might do me good.'

They walked down the hill as a group. The children were excited to be back on their own familiar ground, and excited, too, to have Daniel with them. Anna was on edge but trying hard not to be. She knew how difficult this must be for Daniel, and she wanted to distract him. Stop him worrying and feeling apprehensive.

Besides, she was convinced the problem really was mostly in his own head. His face was horribly scarred, it was true, at least on one side, and people would certainly notice. But only at first, just as they would notice any strange face. Once they had seen him a few times, they would simply accept that that was how it was, what he looked like. Already it had happened to her, and seemingly to the children. Already they were far more concerned with the person behind the face, which was exactly how it should be.

'Where is this village?' Daniel enquired. 'I'm beginning to wonder if it exists.'

'Down there!' Lisa shouted, pointing down the road.

'Down there!' Tom echoed.

Daniel peered doubtfully into the distance. 'I don't know,' he said, shaking his head. 'Do you think we've come the right way?'

'Yes!' Tom screeched.

'I know it's the right way,' Lisa

announced firmly. 'I come down here every day to go to school. At least, I used to,' she qualified, 'before the fire.'

'I don't know,' Daniel mused. 'Maybe you've been away too long. Maybe you've forgotten?'

'Of course I haven't forgotten!'

'Well, I shall have to trust you, Lisa. OK. You're the navigator.'

'It's down there!' Tom yelled again, impatient to be included in any conversation going.

Lisa just smiled now, satisfied. She knew Daniel was teasing.

Anna smiled, too. They were all doing so well, the three of them.

She sensed Daniel tighten up as they passed the first house. It was close to the road, not like the scattered houses they had passed on the hillside. An elderly man was working in the small front garden.

'Hello, George!' Anna called.

The gardener looked up and waved. 'How are you? Sorry to hear about your fire, pet.'

'It could have been worse.'

'Aye, well. You can generally say that about things.'

'This is my next-door neighbour, by the way. Daniel Ferguson, from *Moorside*.'

'Oh? Daniel Ferguson, is it?'

'It is.'

The old man peered closely at Daniel. Anna held her breath until he smiled.

'George Meredith. I've heard about you, lad. Good things. You're the one that saved all their lives, I hear. I'm very pleased to meet you.'

The two of them shook hands. Daniel, embarrassed as he was, even managed to say a couple of words in return.

'There now,' Anna whispered as they walked on. 'That wasn't so bad, was it?'

'I don't know what you mean.'

'No, of course you don't.'

But he smiled. And then he grinned. Anna laughed.

'You can get nearly everything here,'

Anna said as she pushed open the doors to the village shop.

'Especially ice-cream,' Lisa announced. 'Not sweets, though, no,' she added hastily, catching her mother's eye. 'They're bad for you.'

'Not in moderation,' Anna said primly. 'Only in excess.'

'Sweets?' Tom queried. 'I like . . . '

'No, Tom!'

'Hello, Anna!' Rhoda Cummings, the shopkeeper, called. 'Pippa tells me you've moved back up the hill?'

'We have, yes. A long time ago. About two hours, it is now.'

Rhoda laughed.

'There are no secrets in this village,' Anna said for Daniel's benefit.

'Good heavens, no!' Rhoda looked quite indignant.

'Rhoda, this is Daniel Ferguson, our next-door neighbour.'

'You probably won't have seen him before.'

'No. Heard about him, though. Hello, Daniel. You're very welcome here.'

It's going to be all right, Anna thought with relief. Daniel hasn't turned and run. It's going to be all right.

'I can't thank you enough,' he said on the way home.

'For what? There's no need.'

'I would never have got down here myself, on my own. But I'm glad we came. People in the village seem very friendly.'

'Oh, they are.' She smiled and added, 'I hope you'll like it enough to want to stay.'

He looked surprised for a moment. Then he smiled and nodded. 'So do I,' he said.

As the weeks passed, it became to be difficult to recall a time when Daniel did not live next door. Anna grew used to him being there, and was happy about it. It was good to have someone nearby with whom she could comment on the weather or share a joke.

And she liked the way he worked so patiently in his garden, doing what he could, a bit at a time.

She liked to see him growing stronger, too, day by day. She just liked him, she admitted to herself with a wry smile.

The children liked him, too. They were in his garden now even more than in their own. They played again in The Secret Wood, and heard their excited responses.

She heard the laughter and happy voices, and was glad. To think, she thought with another wry smile, how at first they had thought a monster had come to live next door to them.

★   ★   ★

Meanwhile, progress was being made on other fronts, too. Anna passed the theory test for her driving licence and resumed her driving lessons.

Her instructor assured her she would soon be joining the race to the supermarkets in the nearby town.

'You've got the date of your practical

116

test, Anna. You shouldn't have any difficulty. It's a little way off yet. So what you need to do is get some more practice in. Just get more used to the everyday business of being on the road.'

Anna shivered with anticipation. On the road? That sounded wonderful, if still distant.

'Yes,' she said dubiously, wondering how she could get some more practice in.

'With practice,' Kenny intoned solemnly, 'folk become more relaxed, and good drivers are relaxed at the wheel. Alert but relaxed.'

'Yes?' she said again, smiling and thinking it was like being back in school, having someone talking to her like this.

Kenny meant well, though. She knew that. It was just that there were practical matters for her to consider, and practical problems to be overcome.

'Have you got someone who can spend a bit of time with you, while you drive around?'

'Maybe,' she said, thinking there were two of the big practical problems, right there.

'That's good,' he said with approval. 'That's all you need.'

She needed someone to drive with her, and someone to look after Lisa and Tom. Two problems. Pippa and Derek, of course. But there were limits as to how much she could put on them. Another possibility came to mind but she needed to think that through a bit more. She couldn't just ask — or could she?

'If I could drive, I wouldn't have to toil up and down the hill every time I need a loaf of bread.'

'I wondered about that,' Daniel said. 'You don't drive?'

'Not yet, no. It didn't seem necessary when my husband was alive. Rather, I never got around to it. That's more like it. But I'm learning,' she added. 'And once I have my licence, I'll be able to think about a part-time job. That's another thing.'

118

'Good for you. When's your test?'

'Soon. Too soon! I need more practice.'

'Do you need someone to go out with you?'

She looked at him, smiled and nodded. 'Yes, please!'

The day came, surprisingly quickly, when the new kitchen was finished. It was a palace, compared to the old one.

'Oh, Mum!' Lisa breathed. 'It's lovely.'

'It Is, isn't it? We're very lucky.'

She gazed around with happy astonishment. The kitchen was long and narrow still, but its shape was all that was left to remind them of the old kitchen. Close to the connecting door there was a cooker and hob on one side, and a double sink with a window on the other.

At the far end was a breakfasting area they would probably use for most of their meals. It had windows on three sides, and was so light and airy Anna had already decided to have blinds fitted. Otherwise, on a sunny day, it would be like sitting in a greenhouse.

Tom had disappeared for a moment. Now he reappeared, clutching two of his best cars to try out on the tiled floor.

'The far end, Tom, please!' Anna laughed. 'Up here, I'll fall over them.'

Not to be outdone, Lisa brought her colouring book to try out on the new table.

Next, Anna thought happily, I'm going to invite Pippa and Derek for a meal. And I'll ask Daniel, too. It's time they all met properly, and time I gave something back to thank them for what they've done for us.

* * *

'Thank you, Anna. But I can't, I'm afraid.'

'Why ever not?'

'I'm too busy.'

'Too busy?'

'Yes.'

'Pippa and Derek are the friends

120

children and I stayed with in the village. You actually met Derek, I think. Briefly.'

He nodded.

'I thought it would be nice to have you all round to celebrate the opening of the new kitchen. Another time, perhaps, in your case, Daniel. But if your plans change . . . Tomorrow night — about six-thirty? I know it's early, but there's the children. They'd want to see everyone before they go to bed.'

He smiled but she could see he wasn't persuaded. 'I'll have to see,' was the best she could get out of him.

On the way back to her own house she felt irritated and frustrated. And disappointed. He had to engage with people. Why couldn't he see that?

She sighed. One step at a time, she supposed. At least he came down to the village with her sometimes. Quite often, in fact. He wouldn't go into the shop and buy things yet, but he would let her do it for him. And at least he carried the stuff home!

She knew what it was. He still didn't like people seeing him close up. He couldn't bear the thought of them being revolted by sight of his scarred face. Yet it wasn't that bad, his face. And he still had the plastic surgeon to see, with the prospect of further improvement. Anyway, worse things than that had happened to him. More important things. He still wasn't as fit and strong as he must once have been, and as he ought to be again.

But he was getting better. She was in no doubt about that. She'd seen how much easier toiling up the hill was for him now. He was doing well.

'Have you been round to Daniel's, Mum?' Lisa asked when she returned from her fruitless mission next door.

'Yes. I wanted to ask him round for a meal tomorrow, with Pippa and Derek.'

'Oh, good!'

Anna looked at her with surprise, eyebrows raised.

'I like him a lot,' Lisa said with a shrug. 'So does Tom.'

'Good! I'm glad. He's a nice man. Unfortunately, he probably can't come.'

'Oh.' The disappointment was heavy.

'Another time,' Anna said.

'Why can't he come?'

'He's busy, he says.'

'I think it's because he doesn't like meeting people,' Lisa announced. 'He's shy.'

Anna was astonished by her daughter's insight. 'There is a bit of that,' she admitted.

'Because of his wounds,' Lisa declared. 'From the war.'

'War? What war?'

'I don't know. Some war.' Lisa shrugged again. 'He was wounded. You can tell.'

'But people's faces aren't the most important thing about them, Lisa. Not everyone can have a beautiful face.'

'I'm not talking about his face,' Lisa said. 'I'm talking about how he struggles to walk up the hill.'

'Yes, he does still struggle a bit, doesn't he?' Anna admitted. 'He's getting better, though, don't you think?'

'Yes.' Lisa yawned, weary of the subjects now. 'It's because we've been training him.'

'Training him?'

'At football. Me and Tom.'

Anna felt heartened, as well as amused. How she wished Daniel knew how little significance people, even children — especially children! — placed on his scarred face. How she wished he could understand . . . What, exactly? What did she want him to understand? Well . . . How much they cared about him. There, now! She'd said it. They did. They cared about him. And sometimes she felt he cared about them, too.

11

'Oh, I'm so glad you'll both be able to come, Pippa. Poor Derek, though! We'll be tearing him away from his garden for another evening.'

'Don't worry about that. He'll be glad of the break. He's got a bad back, just like he has every year because of the gardening.'

'He must work at it very hard,' Anna said wistfully, gazing out of the window at the perfectly formed rows of cabbages and potatoes, beetroot and peas in Pippa's garden.

'I'd rather have a bigger lawn, frankly — and Derek without a bad back! He's such a grouse when there's anything wrong with him.'

'But you can't beat fresh vegetables. And think of the money you must save.'

'Huh! I don't know about that. By the time he's paid for the special seeds, the various fertilisers, the organic compost — and I don't know what else! — it would be cheaper to buy the vegetables from the shop. Besides, I don't like slug holes in every potato, and the kids don't like caterpillars in the lettuce either.'

Anna laughed. 'Me thinks you protesteth too much!'

'Probably.'

'Oh, I nearly forgot. I've invited Daniel round for the meal, as well. Hope you don't mind?'

'Of course not. The mystery man from next door, eh? I'll look forward to meeting him at last.'

'If he comes. I don't think he will, though.'

'Oh?'

'It's not certain anyway. He says he's busy, but I don't know what to think. Lisa thinks he's just shy.'

'Force him to come. I want to hear all about midnight gardening, and the rest of it.'

Anna smiled. She hoped she was

doing the right thing. She didn't want Pippa making fun of Daniel all night — if he came.

'Things must be better between you, if it's got to this stage?' Pippa suggested.

Anna could feel herself blushing. 'You can just get that twinkle out of your eye, Pippa! I know what you're thinking. Daniel's my neighbour. That's all. There's nothing going on.'

'That's a pity.'

Pippa started laughing. After a moment, reluctantly, Anna joined in.

'Seriously, though,' Pippa added, 'how are you getting on with him?'

'Very well, now. He's a nice man. He's helping me get some driving practice, apart from anything else.'

'Oh?'

'It's good for both of us, I think.'

She went on to explain how and why Daniel was so shy and reclusive, and how she had been trying to get him out of the house more.

'So it's his face he's worried about?'

'Yes. He's still recovering from other injuries, as well. More serious ones, actually. Lung damage, for example. But he's worried that his facial disfigurement will make people stare at him. And perhaps frighten them, especially children.' She paused and added, 'I think he just hates how he looks now.'

'Is it really bad?'

'Well . . . To be honest, Pippa, I suppose it is. On one side, anyway. But I'm used to it now. So are the children. We don't notice it any more.'

'Does it bother Lisa and Tom?'

'No.' She shook her head. 'They like him a lot. So do I, actually. He's a good man. A brave one, too.'

'What about his other injuries?'

'As I said, he's recovering from them. Getting stronger every day. He has to be. We drag him up and down the hill to the shops every day!'

Pippa laughed and shook her head. 'You're doing very well, then, Anna.'

'Me?'

'You and the children. Seeing him. Taking him down to the village. It's the best thing that could have happened to him. To you, too, probably. You needed a friend next door as much as he did.'

Anna wasn't sure what Pippa meant at first but later she realised there was something in what she'd said. They were all helping each other, which was as it should be.

Pippa gasped and her hand flew to her face as soon as she saw the new kitchen. 'It's wonderful,' she said with astonishment. 'Oh, my goodness!'

Anna smiled and didn't even bother to agree.

Pippa spun round. 'Derek, we're setting fire to our kitchen as soon as we get home. I want one of those!'

'It makes you think, doesn't it?' Derek looked round appreciatively. 'Mind you, there was a bit of hassle involved in getting this one. Could you put up with that, my dear?'

'Easily,' Pippa said, giving Anna a wink.

'It has worked out well, in the end, I suppose,' Anna admitted. 'But it's been a dangerous way to go about it. If you really want a new kitchen, Pippa, I'd advise you to get it a more conventional way.'

'And what about . . . Daniel? Has he recovered from the fire?'

'I'm not sure. He says he has. I hope he has.' Anna glanced at the clock. 'It looks as though he won't make it. We'd better make a start.'

'Oh, that's a pity. I'm one of the few people who haven't met him yet.'

'And I was looking forward to seeing him again,' Derek said. 'Our only other meeting was a bit of a breathless encounter.'

Anna was disappointed, too. As she urged her visitors to sit down at the table, she couldn't help wishing a certain other person had been present as well.

'Mum!' Lisa called moments later. 'Mum, can you come and help me, please?'

Anna groaned. 'Excuse me a moment. Derek, can you pour the wine, please?'

She hurried into the hall. 'What is it, Lisa?'

She stopped, confronted by the sight of Lisa wielding a huge bunch of flowers.

'Look what he's brought!'

'Who . . . ?' Anna's eyes moved past the flowers and Lisa. 'Daniel!'

'Not absolutely too late, I hope?'

'Of course not,' she assured him, reaching forward to kiss his cheek.

Too late, aghast, she thought, Oh! What am I doing?

But Daniel just smiled.

'Mum! They're heavy,' Lisa complained.

'Into the kitchen with them. Daniel, come and meet my other guests.'

'Daniel Ferguson,' Anna said proudly. 'Here he is, Pippa. He's come after all.'

It went well from the start. Derek stood up to shake Daniel's hand. Pippa gave him one of her very best smiles. And Daniel . . . Daniel was fun.

'Sorry I'm late everyone. I got lost.'

'Oh, Daniel!' Anna protested, laughing.

'It's easy done,' Pippa pointed out. 'Isn't it, Derek?'

'Easy,' Derek agreed. 'Many's the time, coming back from The Original Oak, I've lost my way.'

'Sometimes,' Daniel said portentously, 'a man just needs help.'

'Spot on!' Derek agreed.

'I'll bring the rice,' Anna announced, hurrying away.

'So, Daniel, you're leaving the Army?' Derek said. 'Or you've already left. Any plans?'

'First to get well again. Then to enjoy my life here.'

'Sounds good to me.'

'You're going to stay?' Pippa asked.

'Oh, yes.' He threw Anna a smile. 'If my neighbours will let me, that is.'

'That's asking a lot,' Anna said.

'I know, I know! You have a lot to put up with.'

'Well,' Pippa said, 'if you get chucked out, move into the village. We're very friendly down there — not like these snobbish folk up on the hill.'

'Army pension good enough to live on?' Derek asked.

'Derek!' Pippa protested.

'Certainly,' Daniel said. 'Better than you'll get eventually from local government, I would think.'

'That wouldn't be hard! Anyway you chaps certainly earn it.'

'But I plan to work for a living anyway.'

'Oh?' Pippa said. 'Get a job, you mean?'

'Start a business.'

'Really?'

'I have half a mind to open a shop.'

'Selling what?'

'Fishing rods.'

'Are you serious?' Anna asked.

'Absolutely. I've noticed Branton doesn't have many shops like that.'

'Hardly any,' Derek agreed.

Pippa began to laugh. After taking a moment to recover, Anna went for the rhubarb crumble.

* * *

The next morning Anna ran into Pippa
in the village shop.

'We really enjoyed last night, Anna.'

'Good. So did I.'

They peered at the vegetables together.
Pippa grimaced. 'They're not up to
much, are they?' Anna whispered with
resignation, gazing at the baskets of
tired carrots and shrivelled cabbages.

'Terrible! And so pricey, too. I wish
I'd asked Derek to get some in town. I
bet you're looking forward to being able
to drive to the supermarket.'

'They have a lot better choice, don't
they? But the money I save on the veg,
I'll probably spend on the petrol.'

'That's true. Anyway, we have to buy
some things here. We've got to keep
Rhoda going. Otherwise, there won't be
a village shop when we want that extra
loaf or we've run out of milk.'

They wandered on to the canned
vegetable shelf. Baked beans or mushy
peas, Anna wondered. Or sweetcorn?

'You've been a naughty girl!' Pippa whispered fiercely.

'Me? What have I done?'

'Keeping secrets.'

'I don't have any secrets to keep, Pippa, and I wouldn't be able to keep them from you for long even if I had some.'

Pippa shook her head. 'You didn't tell me.'

'About what?'

'Daniel Ferguson.'

Anna stared at her.

'Daniel Ferguson,' Pippa repeated. 'You didn't tell me what a lovely man he is.'

'Pippa! Every time I've seen you, I've . . . I'm sure I have!'

'No, you haven't. You've only told me about his injuries, and before that about his dreadful habits — gardening in the night, and so on.'

'Well, I told you how brave he is. You know what he did for us when the kitchen caught fire.'

Pippa picked up a tin of marrowfat

peas and peered ostentatiously at it.

'What?' Anna asked.

'Horrible things, these, but Derek and the kids seem to like them. Personally, I wonder if there's any difference between marrowfat and mushy. What do you think?'

'I'll crown you, Pippa, if you don't stop playing games. What on earth did you mean about Daniel?'

'Well . . . You didn't tell me how fond you are of him, and you didn't tell me how infatuated he is with you.'

Anna stared, unable to think, let alone reply.

'You're a lucky girl, Anna. He's a lovely man.'

'Oh, Pippa! What absolute rubbish you talk at times.'

Pippa laughed. 'Don't tell me if you don't want to. That's all right. Don't tell me anything. I just wanted to say I'm pleased for you.'

'I'm a widow, for goodness' sake, Pippa — with two young children!'

'I'm pleased for you,' Pippa repeated, turning away to head for the fresh

136

bread shelf, where she was far too late to be lucky.

Anna stared after her, and wondered if it could possibly be true. Was Pippa right?

Well, she had to acknowledge, Pippa was right about one thing. She did like Daniel. She really did. Pippa was right about him being a lovely man, too. He was.

But that was as far as it went. She had tried not to let herself think about Daniel as anything but a neighbour and a friend. And a hero, she reminded herself with a wry smile. A wounded hero, at that.

She was drawn to him. She knew that. But it hadn't occurred to her to think that her feelings might be reciprocated. She hadn't dared. Since she'd been left on her own, she had always assumed that that part of her life was over. Besides, she'd been too busy.

Now she wondered. She thought about what Pippa had said. She wondered if there was any way Pippa could possibly be right, and she wondered if she wanted her to be right. It was as if her world was turning upside-down — and she felt exhilarated about it.

12

But there were other matters pressing hard. The driving test was one. And looking for a job was another.

Daniel accompanied her to the test centre when the big day came. She drove carefully and concentrated hard.

'Relax!' he told her. 'You've nothing to worry about.'

'You don't think so?'

He shook his head. 'Outside of a *Challenger Main Battle Tank* I've never had such a comfortable ride.'

'Oh, you!'

But it worked. It made her laugh, and laughing relaxed her.

'They want you to pass,' Daniel told her. 'They don't want to fail you. Just do what you do every day I come out with you, and you'll be fine.'

When she emerged from the test centre, Daniel took one look at her face and said, 'I don't need to ask, do I?'

She laughed and shook her head. He gave her a hug.

'What now?' he asked.

'Next I'm going to talk to a man about a job.'

'Oh?' he looked at her with surprise.

She gave her old boss, Mr Graham, a ring at the bank and had a good chat with him.

'Come in, Anna! Come in to see us — any time.'

'I can, now I've passed my driving test.'

'Excellent. We'll be pleased to see you.'

'I assumed you would have forgotten all about me by now? It's been so long . . .'

'Nonsense!'

Mr Graham went on to say that she knew most of the staff, and they certainly remembered her. They had all been desperately sorry to learn about poor Bob. In fact, only the other day Marion had wondered how she was getting on. She thanked him and assured him that she and the children were all well and getting on happily with their lives.

'And you say there might be a possibility of a part-time job?' she queried.

'Very much so. A lot of the staff work here part-time now, and we're always in need of an experienced pair of hands. Come in. We can talk about it.'

She thanked him again, promised she would go to see them all very soon and rang off in a state of high elation.

'More good news?' Daniel enquired.

'Oh, yes!' she assured him with a smile. 'Very good news. They want me.'

'Of course they do. I could have told you that. No need to go wasting money on a phone call.'

'What a day it's been, Daniel!' She laughed and shook her head. 'First my driving test. Then this. And a lot of it is down to you. How can I ever thank you?'

'And the day has hardly started,'

Daniel pointed out. 'We still have time for a celebratory lunch somewhere.'

'Oh, Daniel?'

'My treat.'

'Oh, Daniel!'

They found a pleasant little restaurant in a nearby village and settled down to lunch.

'My, oh my!' Anna breathed. 'What a day. What a lucky person I am.'

'I don't know about that, about luck. Deserving, maybe.'

She laughed. 'What about you, Daniel? When's something good going to happen to you?'

'I think it already has.'

She let that go. He probably just meant he'd survived his accident and his injuries. That was certainly 'good' enough. He couldn't possibly mean . . .

'What about the shop selling fishing rods? Is that really going to happen?'

'I think so,' he said, toying with his water glass. 'Probably.'

'You were serious?'

'Almost. I have to do something, and

I quite fancy that.'

'Are you a keen fisherman? Or angler? Whatever they call them.'

He shook his head.

'No?'

'I know nothing about it.'

'Oh, Daniel!' She laughed out aloud.

'But I can learn. And at the very least, I can be a great armchair fisherman, especially in the winter. A roaring fire. Coffee pot on the go. Whisky bottle on the shelf. The shop will be a home for people who want to examine the next season's must-have gear, and to talk about the biggest fish they ever hooked.'

'And how it got away?'

'Exactly.' He smiled and added, 'I believe we understand each other, Anna.'

'I believe we do,' she admitted. 'You're a romantic.'

'Absolutely.'

She began to laugh. He joined in. Their laughter filled the room. An elderly couple on the far side looked at

143

each other and began to smile.

It was hot that day, hotter than for a long time. The hottest day of the year. Anna could feel the heat gathering when she first woke up. She glanced at the bedside clock. Six-thirty. Too early to get up. She would just lie here. Give herself five minutes. Ten even. Think about the day ahead.

First she would do an hour in the garden. It was lovely first thing at this time of year. Then she would get the children up and sort out breakfast. Put a load of washing in the machine. Take down the stuff left to dry overnight.

Then . . . ? Then she would ask Daniel if he fancied a day at the beach with herself and the children. If Pippa was right, and she was daring to hope she might be, he couldn't say no. Could he?

It would be good for them all. And the drive — with him beside her, and her with her new driving licence! — would be good practical experience. She'd only been local so far.

Action plan formed, eager to get on with it, she sprang out of bed and tackled the day with zest. This was going to be one of the best days of her life. She was certain of it, and determined to make sure it was.

Just after nine she set off for Daniel's. The children were just as excited as she was herself. All that remained was to persuade Daniel that it was time to see some sand and sea. It shouldn't be too hard.

A car pulled into Daniel's gateway as she reached her own front gate, a strange car. She paused, uncertain whether to go on.

A woman she had never seen before got out and strode towards the door. She was tall and slim. Long, dark hair. Thirty-ish. Slender white arms swinging from a sleeveless black top. Long, tanned legs clad in white bermudas.

Anna was surprised, and curious. Who on earth was she? Daniel didn't have visitors like this. Daniel didn't have any visitors at all, in fact, apart from his increasingly occasional sister.

She inspected the gate. She bent down and pulled out an easy weed. She was flummoxed. She'd better wait. Hopefully, the woman would soon leave. Perhaps she'd come to read the electricity meter? Or to tell Daniel he'd won the Jackpot? Perhaps . . .

It wasn't funny. She had no idea who the woman was. She would wait. There was nothing else she could do.

'Can Daniel go?' Lisa demanded as soon as she reached the safety of her own doorway.

'I don't know yet, Lisa. I haven't seen him.'

'But . . .'

'A visitor arrived just as I was about to go round. We'll have to wait for her to leave.'

She turned and laughed at Tom, who was standing there all ready to go, bucket and spade retrieved miraculously from some forgotten corner.

'Not yet, Tom! We're not ready yet.'

The strange car was still there at nine-thirty, and even at ten. Perhaps, Anna thought, the woman is from the Army Benevolent Fund, or whatever they called it, come to see officially how Daniel is?

It wasn't a very convincing thought. The strange woman had seemed too beautiful for anything like that. Also, she told herself cheerfully, she hadn't been wearing khaki, or any of those camouflage patterns Army people seemed to wear these days.

At ten-forty she saw the woman take a small suitcase from the car and carry it into Daniel's house.

She felt then as if the bottom had dropped out of her life.

Soon after eleven Anna set off for the village, a sullen Lisa and protesting Tom in tow. She herself felt utterly miserable but she fought to escape the despair that had engulfed them all.

'Another day, Tom!' she said as cheerfully as she could manage. 'We'll go to the beach another day.'

'Now!' Tom screeched. 'Want to go now.'

'Sorry, darling. We really need to do some shopping. Silly Mummy had forgotten we need some bread — and some milk.'

'Don't want any bread!' howled Tom.

'Ice-cream, then?'

Even that didn't have any immediate effect. Anna kept a tight hold of his hand and pulled him along.

'I'm sorry, Lisa,' she said. 'I should have arranged it with Daniel before I mentioned it to you and got you all excited.'

'Doesn't matter.'

'We can go another day.'

'I don't care.'

Privately, Anna thought that was probably the best way to think. You could avoid more disappointment that way. And from the appearance of Daniel's visitor, there would be a lot more disappointment to come.

Oh, damn Pippa! Putting such ideas into her head. What on earth had allowed her to be persuaded Daniel could ever be interested in her?

'We'll go to Pippa's, and you can play with the boys while I do a bit of shopping.'

'I don't care,' Lisa repeated stubbornly.

Pulling them all out of this mood was going to be an uphill struggle, Anna decided grimly.

'What's wrong?' Pippa said straightaway.

'Wrong? Nothing. Nothing at all.' Anna summoned up her limited reserves of positive feelings and good humour. 'What a wonderful day it is!'

'Yes?' Pippa said doubtfully, as she ushered them into the house.

'It would be a good day to go to the beach.'

'Oh, don't say that!' Anna groaned, as Tom started wailing again. 'That's what we were going to do.'

'Where's David and Peter?' Lisa asked.

'In the garden. Why don't you go and

find them? You, too, Tom. Now,' Pippa said. 'What's wrong? Just one of those days, or . . . ?'

Anna shrugged.

In the end, over a cup of coffee, she told Pippa of their thwarted plan, and of her own disappointment.

'He's never mentioned a woman,' she concluded. 'On the other hand, he's never made advances to me either. So I should have guessed.'

'Not that he would,' she added hastily. 'And not that I'm the sort of woman likely to attract them anyway. I mean . . .'

'Of course you are! Stop putting yourself down.'

Anna looked down at her hands and concentrated on them. She felt tears coming to the surface. Then she felt Pippa's arms go round her.

'Oh, Anna! I'm so sorry. What a wretched morning you've had.'

'It's the children I'm upset about. I promised them . . . Now we can't . . .'

But it was herself, as well, she felt

sorry for. She knew that.

'It may mean nothing,' Pippa suggested. 'Maybe she was selling insurance or kitchens. He's seen your new kitchen, and now he wants one. It's perfectly understandable.'

'Oh, Pippa! Stop it.'

But she had to smile at the idea. 'You haven't seen her, Pippa. She's very beautiful.'

'So are you very good looking. I mean . . . beautiful.'

'Stop it!' Anna repeated.

'Anyway,' Pippa added, 'it doesn't mean . . . '

'Pippa, she took a suitcase into the house!'

'His sister, maybe?'

'I've met his sister. She's called Elizabeth, remember? And she's Miss Jean Brodie in person.'

Even Pippa had to laugh now.

'What I'll do,' Anna announced, 'so it's not a totally wasted morning, is I'll go to the shop and pick up a few things we need.'

'If only my car hadn't fallen apart,' Pippa said, 'we could have gone to the beach in that. We only have the one car at the moment, though. We could take yours, I suppose? All go in that?'

'Not six of us,' Anna said firmly. 'It doesn't matter anyway. Don't worry about it. I'll just leave the kids here, if you don't mind, while I do a bit of shopping.'

13

Almost the first person Anna saw in the village shop was Daniel's sister. 'Hello, Elizabeth,' she said brightly. 'I haven't seen you for a while.'

'I've not been needed,' Elizabeth replied, equally brightly. 'I'm getting on with my own life.'

'Oh, yes. You have a private school, don't you? Daniel said.'

'Just a little one. But it keeps me busy.'

Her own school, Anna thought. What an extraordinary person she is.

'And how are you, my dear?'

Anna was almost stunned. The question was one she would never have thought Elizabeth capable of asking.

'Very well, thank you. And you?'

'Harassed — even more than usual. You don't have the children with you today?'

153

'Not right now, no. They're with my friend in the village.'

'Giving you time to shop. I know, I know!'

Perhaps she really does, Anna thought. No! She couldn't possibly know what I'm going through.

'Could you spare me a few minutes, dear? I would very much like to talk to you.'

'Yes, of course. I'm not in a hurry.'

'Good. May I offer you a cup of coffee, in the tea shop next door perhaps?'

Anna was too overwhelmed to think of an objection.

They settled themselves in at *Betty's Teashop*. Elizabeth looked around, smiled and, said, 'It may not be quite the same as its namesake in Harrogate, but it's certainly a lot less busy and very much quieter.'

'We'll probably be half their customers today. I don't think they do an awful lot of trade.'

'Really? That's a pity. It's a nice little place.'

While Anna was wondering about the significance of Harrogate, Elizabeth leaned forward and fixed her with a stern expression.

'Are you familiar with *Betty*'s, in Harrogate?'

Anna shook her head.

'Ah! Well, it's a charming old traditional tea shop, much appreciated by people of a certain age, including myself. But I digress.'

Elizabeth paused, and for a moment seemed surprisingly unsure how to continue.

'I am, as you no doubt realise, very concerned for my brother. He's had a bad year, a very bad year. As I told you, he is here to convalesce. I found the house, *Moorside*, for him, and I believed it to be a safe and peaceful place for him to recover his health and strength.'

Oh, dear! Anna thought with a wince. I can see where this is heading.

'Seemingly, I was mistaken,' Elizabeth continued.

'I'm very sorry you feel that way,' Anna said quickly. 'I'm afraid we have disturbed his peace and quiet, it's true, but with the best of intentions. Small children . . . ' She added vaguely. 'And then there was the fire. I . . . '

She broke off in a state of mounting anguish and despair. It was all becoming too much for her. She couldn't just sit here and be told off, not when she had so much on her mind.

'My dear,' Elizabeth said, 'please don't misunderstand me. I am not here to chastise you. On the contrary. I am here to thank you. I'm very grateful to you and your children.'

Anna stared blankly.

'You've lessened my load considerably, if I can put it like that. I've been able to get on with my own life at the school. More important, you've given my brother something to live for, with the result that his recovery has been very much quicker than we had dared to hope.'

'I don't understand. I . . . '

'You like him, don't you?'

'Well, yes. Very much. But . . . '

'And Daniel is very fond of you, my dear. I wanted to tell you that. It might make things easier. Smooth the way, as it were.'

'Ridiculous, isn't it?' Elizabeth added. 'I feel like a Victorian father, not a modern old maid!'

Anna smiled uncertainly. 'Daniel hasn't said anything to me,' she began tentatively. 'I mean, I like him a lot. The children do, as well. But that's as far as our . . . our relationship goes.'

'How could he say anything?' Elizabeth said brusquely. 'With his injuries, he assumed no-one would be interested in him ever again. Nonsense, of course. But there you are. He's had a bad time. And that fiancée of his didn't help either. What a wicked woman!'

For a moment the words failed to register. 'Fiancée? What do you mean, Elizabeth?'

'Hasn't he told you?' When Anna shook her head, Elizabeth tut-tutted and resumed. 'Daniel was engaged to be married. After he was wounded, that woman took one look at him and announced their engagement was over. She couldn't bear to look at him, and told him so.'

'But that's terrible!'

Elizabeth nodded. 'I told him he was well out of it. A woman capable of thinking and feeling like that wasn't one to marry.'

'Poor man! How awful.'

'He pretended not to be bothered, of course, the way men like him do. He keeps his emotions well hidden, as a professional soldier must. But I know he felt it deeply. As if his injuries were not enough! He became more depressed than ever.'

Anna grimaced. Poor Daniel!

'It wasn't until he met you that he came out of it,' Elizabeth continued. 'He's been much more like his old self, his real self, lately. It's thanks to you, my dear. What is it?' she added, breaking off. 'You don't seem very happy about what I've told you.'

'Oh, I'm sorry. I'm very pleased for Daniel, I really am. But . . . '

'But?'

'The truth is, Elizabeth, that I was beginning to hope Daniel and I might in time become more than just good friends. Until today, that is.'

'Why? What's special about today?'

'A woman arrived this morning at Daniel's.' She shrugged and added, 'A young woman, with a suitcase.'

'Oh, she's here already, is she?' Elizabeth's face assumed a grim expression. 'I knew she was coming, of course. That's why I'm here.'

Anna stared.

'It's Shona. His ex-fiancée. Come on! Drink up. I must get up there.'

'What is it, Elizabeth? I don't understand.'

'That woman announced that she was coming to see him. She wasn't invited, mark you! She simply wrote and told Daniel she was coming. Presumably to see if his appearance had improved, and he might be worth marrying, after all.'

'You can't be serious?'

'Oh, I am! Daniel has money, you see. Inherited family money. And Shona is well aware of it. She wouldn't want to give that up if she could possibly help it. Now I must go and make my thoughts and feelings known to her.'

Daniel's visitor was emerging from the house as Anna neared the top of the hill with the children. She marched to her car, flung open a door and hurled the suitcase inside.

Oh, dear! Anna thought. It doesn't look as though the visits gone very well. Good!

'Keep up, Tom!' she called. 'We're nearly there.'

Then Anna's arm was nearly dead from hurtling backwards out of the driveway. Anna stopped and held tight on to the children's hands.

'Wow!' Lisa gasped, clearly impressed.

Tom's head jerked up.

The shuddering noise of wheels

spinning on loose gravel was hard to ignore. Anna did her best.

But the woman called to her through the open window. 'Are you the person who lives next door?'

'Yes.'

'Well, he's all yours. And the very best of luck — you're going to need it!'

With that, she floored the accelerator and took off, her rear wheels showering them all with gravel. Anna could only stare, aghast.

When she looked round again, she saw Daniel coming down the steps at the front of his house. She gave Lisa the front door key. 'You and Tom go on, Lisa. I just want to have a quick work with Daniel.'

14

He took forever to reach the front gate. She wasn't sure. She knew she wanted to say something, but she didn't know what. So she stood still and waited.

'Are you all right?' Daniel called as he approached.

She nodded. 'And you?'

'Crazy woman!' he muttered, shaking his head. 'Driving like that. She's going to kill someone.'

'You, perhaps?'

He shrugged. 'Probably.'

'I would guess she's in a bad mood.'

'That's about right.'

He seemed distracted. It wasn't surprising. Things had obviously been said.

'Have you got a minute?' he asked. 'To come in?'

'Is Elizabeth there?'

'No. She's gone. I fight my own

battles. They've both gone now.'

'She gave him a rueful smile and let him lead her into the house, and into the kitchen.'

'That was my ex-fiancée,' he said bluntly.

'Elizabeth told me.'

'I daresay she did. The interfering so-and-so! Probably a lot of other things, too. Elizabeth means well but she should be more careful with other people's private business.'

They were both stood up. Daniel turned to look out of the window, and then back to look at Anna again. He smiled suddenly.

'I was in a poor state when I came here,' he said quietly. 'You know that. Some of it was due to Shona, there, who has just departed in such a great hurry. She took one look at me in hospital and announced that she couldn't marry me. She was brave, too. She told me to my face — what was left of it!'

While you were no doubt covered in bandages and strapped to a bed, Anna thought. Very brave. 'That was good of her.'

He shrugged. 'Turned out it was one of the best things that ever happened to me. Can you imagine how it might have been in five years' time had I married her? In ten years' time — twenty?'

'Not easily,' Anna admitted with a reluctant smile of her own.

'Hell on earth, probably!' Daniel grinned and seemed to relax at last.

'She changed her mind when she heard I was getting well again. And this,' he added, fingering his scarred face, 'wasn't as bad as it might have been.'

'Oh, Daniel! It's so sad.'

'She announced that she was coming. I couldn't stop her. Mistakenly, I confided in Elizabeth. Told her the problem. Elizabeth decided she would come, too. Women!' he added, shaking his head.

'We're not all a nuisance, you know.'

'No, of course you're not.' He smiled and touched her hand. 'Anyway, I've sent her packing, with a few home truths of my own. She wasn't best pleased.'

'So I gathered.'

'Cup of coffee? Tea?'

She shook her head. 'I must get back to the children.'

'Something else I wanted to tell you, Anna, is that one of the best things to have happened to me was . . . '

'Apart from Shona telling you she no longer wanted to marry you?'

'Apart from that.' He paused, and gave a little shrug. 'Was meeting you, Anna. You saved my life. I truly believe that.'

It was a shock, hearing that bald statement. She blinked hard.

'I care for you very much, Anna. And for the children. I told Shona that, as well.'

She stood still.

'It's not easy for me to talk about such things,' he added.

'You don't really need to,' she said softly.

'I don't have the right words.'

'Doesn't matter.'

'I always assumed you couldn't possibly feel the same way about me. I just assumed . . . Anyway, Elizabeth suggested I might be wrong.'

'You were. You were wrong.'

'Really?' He looked at her slowly, head slightly to one side, beginning to smile again.

She nodded happily and moved towards him. He wrapped his arms around her.

'Really!' she confirmed.

She looked up, and at last he kissed her.

THE END

We do hope that you have enjoyed reading this large print book.

Did you know that all of our titles are available for purchase?

We publish a wide range of high quality large print books including:
Romances, Mysteries, Classics
General Fiction
Non Fiction and Westerns

Special interest titles available in large print are:
The Little Oxford Dictionary
Music Book, Song Book
Hymn Book, Service Book

Also available from us courtesy of Oxford University Press:
Young Readers' Dictionary
(large print edition)
Young Readers' Thesaurus
(large print edition)

For further information or a free brochure, please contact us at:
Ulverscroft Large Print Books Ltd.,
The Green, Bradgate Road, Anstey,
Leicester, LE7 7FU, England.
Tel: (00 44) **0116 236 4325**
Fax: (00 44) **0116 234 0205**

FELICITY MOON

Valerie Holmes

When, in self defence, Felicity Moon strikes her employer Julian Cannon, she is forced to leave the place where her father had sent her for her own safety. Accused and jailed for bank-rolling smugglers, Squire Moon is unaware of the dangers Felicity is facing. She is given one last chance by Cannon's housekeeper in the form of a reference to Mr Lucas Packman, a man her father distrusts. Felicity faces a stark choice: trust Packman or her father.

ELUSIVE LOVE

Karen Abbott

Amelia has always been determined to marry for love . . . but with her elder brother dead and post-humously branded as a traitor, Amelia and her sister find themselves penniless and ostracised by society. When a relative contrives to put an *'eligible parti'* under an obligation to make Amelia an offer, Amelia has to decide whether or not to stand by her principles . . . and face the consequences of turning down what might be her only chance to escape her unbearable situation.

THE LEGACY OF THE TOWER

Sheila Lewis

Lizanne Naismith is saddened when Jeffrey Falkin, owner of her former ancestral home, Gilliestoun Tower, dies in an accident. The grief of his family turns to shock and denial when an unknown son, Alex, turns up. Lizanne is the only one to befriend him, much to the chagrin of her boyfriend Steven, Jeffrey's son. Using her skills as a researcher she investigates Alex's mysterious background. When a long-buried secret is revealed, it alters the lives of everyone involved.